STARRY
RIVER
OF THE
SKY

STARRY
RIVER
OF THE
SKY

 Grace Lin

LITTLE, BROWN AND COMPANY
NEW YORK BOSTON

Little, Brown and Company

Hachette Book Group
1290 Avenue of the Americas, New York, NY 10104
Visit our website at www.lb-kids.com

Little, Brown and Company is a division of Hachette Book Group, Inc.
The Little, Brown name and logo are trademarks of Hachette Book Group, Inc.

The publisher is not responsible for websites (or their content) that are not owned by the publisher.

First Paperback Edition: February 2014
First published in hardcover in October 2012 by Little, Brown and Company

Library of Congress Cataloging-in-Publication Data

Lin, Grace.
    Starry River of the Sky / by Grace Lin. — 1st ed.
        p. cm.
    Companion book to: Where the mountain meets the moon.
    Summary: An innkeeper's chore boy discovers that a visitor's stories hold the key to returning the moon to the Starry River of the Sky.
    ISBN 978-0-316-12595-6 (hc) / ISBN 978-0-316-12597-0 (pb)
    [1. Fairy tales.   2. Moon — Fiction.   3. Storytelling — Fiction.]   I. Title.
    PZ8.L6215St 2012
    [Fic] — dc23

                                                                        2012012651

10 9 8 7 6 5 4

SC

Book design by Alison Impey

Printed in China

FOR KI-KI

SPECIAL THANKS TO:

ALEX, ALVINA, BETHANY, LIBBY, AND REBECCA

CHAPTER

1

Rendi was not sure how long the moon had been missing. He knew only that for weeks, the wind seemed to be whimpering as if the sky were suffering. At first, he had thought the moans were his own because his whole body ached from hiding in the merchant's moving cart. However, it was when the cart had stopped for the evening, when the bumping and knocking had ended, that the groans began.

The sky had moaned and cried for many nights before Rendi finally dared to peek out. When he heard the donkey being led away and the nighttime wails beginning again, Rendi crawled from behind the *gangs* of wine — huge pottery vessels as big as he was — and poked out his head from the covered cart. Yet when he looked up into the sky, he saw nothing. The stars had dimmed to little more than faded shadows, and the mournful noises echoed in the blackness. It was then that Rendi realized the moon was missing.

He thought it would appear the next night, or the night after. Rendi was sure the moon would return, as it always had — glowing as if it were cut from the sky with a pair of sharp scissors. But it did not. Every evening, after the merchant had left, Rendi crept from the stifling, sticky cart into the fresh night air and peeked up. And every time, the Starry River of the Sky was empty.

"You must have wine," a voice said. *The merchant!* In the cart, Rendi froze. Another moonless night had passed, and the darkness inside the covered cart had thinned with the morning's arrival. The hitching of the donkey had jerked Rendi awake, his head knocking against one of the clay vats, but it was the sound of voices that alarmed him. "It is the Day of Five Poisons. I can sell you a *gang*," the smooth voice of the merchant said.

"I own an inn, not a tavern," another voice replied. "I don't need a *gang* of wine. That is too much."

"Ah, but having some wine stocked does not make your place a tavern," the merchant replied. "You offer tea and food in the dining room of your inn, do you not? Offer wine as well, and your guests will gladly pay."

"I just need enough wine to protect us from the Noxious Animals," the innkeeper said. "For me to drink and to write the *wang* symbol on my daughter's forehead. One jug will be fine."

"But it is the famous Son Wine," the merchant said. "And I can give you a very good deal."

"Son Wine?" the innkeeper said. Rendi could hear the hesitation. *Don't buy any!* Rendi begged silently, trying to quiet his thumping heart. *Don't open the cart!*

"I can sell it in the city for a high price, but it has been so hot that I'm afraid the wine may spoil before I get there," the merchant continued. "You can see I've even had to cover my cart. It's better for me to sell you some now. We can include my last night's lodging in the cost."

As noiselessly as possible, Rendi scrambled to the back of the cart while the men outside agreed on a price. Rendi squeezed between the two *gangs* farthest from the opening, the huge clay containers compressing him like meat in a dumpling. The cart opened, and Rendi clasped his bag close to him, feeling the hardness of his rice bowl through the cloth.

The merchant and the innkeeper struggled to remove a *gang*, rocking the cart back and forth. Rendi scarcely breathed, and the men grunted as they pushed and shoved. Neither noticed the small figure well hidden in the shadows of the remaining *gangs*.

With a rude curse from the merchant, the vat finally dropped safely to the ground with a thud. Both men leaned against the cart, and the sun glinted from the back of the merchant's bald, perspiring head. As the innkeeper sighed from the exertion, Rendi slowly let out his breath. *Safe*, Rendi thought as he listened to the men finish their deal. He closed his eyes in relief.

"What's that?" the innkeeper said.

Rendi's eyes flew open. Hands and arms reached toward him, grabbing and pulling. He squirmed and struggled,

but there was no escape. Rendi was roughly dragged out of the cart, and soon he was staggering and squinting in the bright daylight.

"A stowaway!" the merchant growled, his friendly manner disappearing. The merchant was wiry and sun-brown, and his hands were as strong as iron chains. One hand clamped the back of Rendi's neck in a relentless grip while the other rose to strike him with a vicious blow.

Rendi cringed, but the innkeeper grabbed the merchant's arm before it struck. "He's just a boy," said the innkeeper, who was shaped a bit like a jug of wine himself. "He doesn't look much older than my daughter."

"You can have him, then!" the merchant said with an unkind laugh. He shoved Rendi to the ground. As Rendi coughed up dust and the innkeeper helped him to his feet, the merchant quickly closed the cart, climbed into the driver's seat, and grabbed the reins of the donkey. "Didn't you say your son left?" he mocked. "Take this one. He's included with the wine!"

"But..." the innkeeper said as the wheels of the cart spit dust at him. "But..."

Swiftly, the merchant drove away, deaf to the innkeeper's

stammers. The innkeeper gaped from the cart to the boy, and then at the cart again. The boy clung to his cloth bag, and the cart blurred in the distance. The innkeeper stared blankly at it. And when the merchant and his cart finally disappeared into the flat line of the horizon, Master Chao, the innkeeper, was still staring.

CHAPTER

2

Rendi's muscles were as soft as uncooked tofu and his face as friendly as an angry tiger, but Master Chao said finally, "I do need someone to help with the chores at the inn."

A chore boy! Rendi scowled with scorn, but then he saw the long, wide, empty road in front of him and the dust from the merchant's cart floating in the air like a fading ghost. The grass was yellow and withering, and a quick scan around showed, besides the shabby inn, a handful of broken-down stone houses. *There's nothing here!* Rendi thought with shock. *Where am I?*

"What kind of chores?" Rendi said, forcing the words from his mouth. He would stay for now, he told himself. But just for now.

"Well, first," Master Chao said, "I need you to help me bring this wine into the inn."

Rendi was not much help moving the wine. He could not get his puny arms around the *gang*, much less lift it. Master Chao grunted and huffed and panted and had only succeeded in moving the wine a few feet when Rendi said, "If we put it on its side, we could roll it."

Master Chao stopped and said, "What is your name?"

"Rendi."

"Well, Rendi," Master Chao said, "that is a good idea."

Rendi's dark frown lightened. They tilted the *gang* and slowly rolled it into the inn, the hot sun burning their necks. But when they brought the wine into the back storeroom, a small figure ran in like lightning, and Rendi's scowl returned.

It was Master Chao's young daughter, Peiyi. Her round face still showed remains of her breakfast, and the bottoms of her pant legs were brown with dirt. Rendi wrinkled his nose, looking at her as if she were a worm in a half-eaten peach.

"Who's that boy?" Peiyi asked, stopping in midstride.

"That's Rendi," Master Chao said without turning. He was mixing realgar powder into a small bowl of wine. "Rendi is going to take over some of Jiming's chores. Rendi, this is my daughter, Peiyi."

Rendi sniffed and rolled his eyes away from her in contempt. Peiyi's eyes narrowed.

However, Master Chao seemed not to notice and brought Peiyi in front of him. He gently pushed her tangled hair from her cherry-blossom-pink face. She stood as still as a carved statue, with only her eyes moving, as her father dipped his finger into the wine mixture and carefully wrote *wang*, a symbol of power, with it on her forehead. Rendi watched from the doorway, and a strange, jealous anger filled him.

"That should protect you from the Noxious Animals," Master Chao said to her, and sighed. "Day of Five Poisons, already! Spring was hardly here, and now it's summer."

Peiyi didn't answer, for her eyes were glued on Rendi in the doorway. He had been making rude faces at her, pretending to be each of the five poisonous animals — snake, scorpion, centipede, spider, and toad. His last impression

was of the Noxious Toad, which he made by bulging his eyes and sticking out his tongue.

"Why is that boy here?" Peiyi said, her lips pursing.

"I told you," Master Chao said. "With Jiming gone, we need someone to help with the chores."

"We don't need him!" Peiyi protested. "Jiming will come back!"

Master Chao sighed again, this time a heavy sigh that fell like a stone in water. "Your brother made his decision," he said, standing up stiffly. Without another word, Master Chao walked out of the room.

Peiyi stared after her father with forlorn eyes and then looked at Rendi. The strange, jealous anger from before had lingered and strengthened, and he jeered at her.

"Baby!" Rendi said. "Too young to drink the wine, so you have to wear the *wang* sign! Watch out for the Noxious Animals!"

Peiyi glared. "Horrible!" she hissed at him, and ran out of the room.

CHAPTER

3

To Rendi, this small Village of Clear Sky and its inn were horrible. Peiyi was forced to show him everything, and she fumed with anger as he sneered at the rough wooden floors, the humble and broken-down houses, and the yellowing weeds dying between the rocks in the walls.

The only thing Rendi could not scorn was the strange, endless plain of stone that lay beyond the inn. The smooth rock ground stretched beyond sight, as if someone had wiped away part of the landscape with a rag.

"What is that?" Rendi gasped in spite of himself.

"It's the Stone Pancake," Peiyi answered. She was glad there was at least one thing this horrid boy could not mock. "My ancestor made it."

"Made it?" Rendi said in disbelief. "You're lying!"

"It's true!" Peiyi insisted. "My ancestor was a great man."

"*Your* ancestor? *My* ancestor was the..." Rendi sputtered, and then stopped.

"What did your ancestor do?" Peiyi said. "Mine moved a mountain!"

Rendi bit his lip in frustration. His ancestors were far greater than the ancestors of this dirty-faced girl! But he swallowed his words bitterly and, instead, said, "How?"

 # THE STORY OF THE MAN WHO MOVED A MOUNTAIN

hen this place was called the Village of Endless Mountain, my esteemed great-grandfather moved here. He was an

extraordinary man. He was so determined and courageous that when he wanted his tea made of Nan Ling water, he journeyed the hundreds of miles to the Long River and braved the brutal and violent waves to get it. He was so smart and clever that he never lost a game of chess in his entire life. He was so strong and powerful that he pulled two oxen by their tails through the street. So wondrous was my honored great-grandfather that all, even the spirits above, looked upon him with admiration.

So, when one fall morning he looked out his window and was displeased, the ground seemed to join his family with their trembling. "I see nothing out my window," my great-grandfather cried. "Why can I not see the sky, the sun, and clouds?"

"Honored father" — his two sons and wife bowed at his feet —"our house is next to the mountain. You do not see the sky in your room, because the mountain blocks it."

My esteemed great-grandfather sputtered, "I must be able to see the sky! I cannot let the mountain block the heavens! We will move the mountain."

He gathered shovels and pails, and he and his obedient sons began to dig. One bucket at a time, they began to carry the mountain away. Obviously, this seemed an impossible task, like emptying the ocean with a rice bowl. Yet my honored great-grandfather was not discouraged, and day after day, he and his sons carried away buckets of earth.

All the villagers came to watch in amazement as my great-grandfather and his sons attempted to move the mountain. Their awed whispers carried to the clouds, and the Spirit of the Mountain overheard. The Spirit gazed down at my great-grandfather and his tireless, unyielding shoulders bearing away stones of the mountain and was alarmed. The Spirit took human form and rushed down.

"Why are you trying to move the mountain?" the Spirit asked my honored great-grandfather. "To carry it away, bucket by bucket — is that not impossible? Even if you were to live a hundred years and work every day, you could not achieve it."

My esteemed great-grandfather brushed away the words. "I will move this mountain," he said. "If I do not move the mountain in my lifetime, my sons will continue my work and their sons after that. Eventually, this mountain of annoyance will be gone!"

The Mountain Spirit heard the truth in my honored great-grandfather's words and began to quake and shiver with fear. Without another word, the Spirit left. The next morning, the sun streamed into my great-grandfather's room. He leaped from his bed and ran outside.

The mountain was gone.

Instead, there was an empty stone field that seemed as flat as a plate and as endless as the sky. My honored great-grandfather stood with pride. He had moved the mountain.

"And that is why we have the Stone Pancake," Peiyi finished. "It is where the mountain used to be, before it fled from my great-grandfather's power and wisdom."

"No one uses it?" Rendi said.

"Nothing grows on it, no one builds on it, and no one travels on it," Peiyi said, shaking her head. "It's so big that if you walk on it far enough, you'll see nothing but the sky and the flat stone and get lost! Sometimes we use a small bit of it near the inn for celebrations, like weddings, but usually it is left bare."

"I can't believe it," Rendi said. But the never-ending flat land drew out in front of him, and he could think of no other explanation.

"The missing mountain is also why this place is called the Village of Clear Sky," Peiyi couldn't help adding. "Because the sky is clear of the mountain."

Clear of the moon too, Rendi thought grimly.

That evening, in his new bedroom at the inn, the moans of the sky returned. Rendi clenched his teeth and covered his ears with his hands until, finally, he glared out his window into the dark. Below the groaning of the night, he heard the satisfied snores coming from the bedroom of Master Chao. Was Rendi the only one who heard the sky? Was it just in his head? Why wouldn't it leave him alone? Another cry echoed.

"Stop it!" Rendi whispered fiercely into the moonless sky. "I'm not going to listen to your whining anymore!"

But the night just gave a mournful noise in answer, and

Rendi scowled. He would forget about the sobbing sky, the missing moon, everything. He would forget it all. He turned from the window, shutting his eyes. There was nothing to see anyway. Outside, there was only blackness and the poor Village of Clear Sky.

CHAPTER

4

Just like that, Rendi became the chore boy at the Inn of Clear Sky. He was not used to doing chores, so when he found a broom in his hand, he had to watch Peiyi to learn how to sweep. He watched her so closely as she washed and dusted that she was convinced he was mocking her and said in annoyance, "Go clean that room by yourself."

As he left, Peiyi added, "Do a good job. It's the best room in the inn."

Just by her tone, Rendi could tell that the room was a point of pride. Instead of plain wood, the couch bed in this room was carved with ribbon-tailed birds and plum blossoms. There was a matching table, and the warm-colored wood shone as if it had just been dipped in honey. Silk scrolls hung on the wall, and lacquered, painted gourds stood as vases.

Rendi sneered. "Best room in the inn," he scoffed to one of the painted peonies. "It's not even good enough for one of my father's servants."

But as the words fell from his lips, he froze and his face darkened. Without another word, Rendi spent the rest of the time vigorously polishing and dusting, flinging the dirt from the window as if to rid the room of any of his lingering words. When he finished, the room was spotless, and even Peiyi could not find any fault with it.

Wasted work, though, Rendi often thought. With the exception of old Mr. Shan, who did not even stay at the inn but just came to eat every day, there were no guests at the Inn of Clear Sky. Rendi watched carefully day after day, hoping another merchant or trader would arrive so he could leave this poor, pitiful village with its crying sky.

It could barely be called a village, really; most of the homes were empty and abandoned, and the people who lived here now would barely fill the dining room of the inn. "Everyone leaves. Villagers, guests, everyone. Even my brother left," Peiyi had said sadly to Rendi. But she had added with a note of happiness, "Even you'll go, someday."

I hope someday soon, Rendi had thought.

But it was not to be today. In the morning, Rendi awoke to the strident crow of the neighbor's rooster and looked out the window. As he expected, the hot sun shone brightly on the undisturbed yard, and there was not a horse or hoofprint visible. Rendi sighed and washed his face. Perhaps tomorrow a guest would come. A guest with a cart he could crawl into.

"You're late," Master Chao said as Rendi and Peiyi walked down the stairs. "We have a new guest."

"A new guest?" Peiyi said in surprise. Rendi was also surprised. The sky's moaning had kept him awake most of the night, and he had heard no one arrive. "Did he come in the night?"

"No," Master Chao said. "Arrived early this morning, alone, on foot, and paid for a room for a whole month. She said she may stay longer."

"She?" Rendi said. The word spurted from him in surprise. It was unheard of for a woman to be staying alone at an inn, much less one who came on foot and stayed for longer than a night.

"Yes," Master Chao said, "and she wants her breakfast brought to her room. Make sure you ask her if she wants all her meals there."

"What is she doing here?" Peiyi asked. "And for so long?"

"That's not our business," Master Chao said, quickly shaking his head at Peiyi. "She paid for her room and meals. That is all that concerns us."

Peiyi looked at Rendi, but he did not return her gaze. He hoped he looked bored and uninterested, even though inside he was as curious as she was.

CHAPTER
5

"I'll help you bring up the breakfast," Peiyi said to Rendi. He wasn't fooled. He knew she just wanted to peek at their new, mysterious guest. But he said nothing and handed her the covered cup of tea.

The new female guest was standing at the window in the finest room of the inn, the same window Rendi had flung dust out of. Her back was toward them, and she stood against the yellow sunlight. The darkness of her silhouette reminded Rendi of the moonless sky that cried at him at night.

"Your breakfast," Rendi said, "Madame..."

"Madame Chang," the woman said. Her serene voice seemed out of place in the hot room, already baking in the summer sun. "Tell me," Madame Chang said without turning, "what did you name the stone field where the mountain was?"

"The Stone Pancake," Peiyi said, pleased that this new guest already knew the story. "It was my ancestor who moved the mountain!"

"Really?" Madame Chang said, and she turned and looked at them. Rendi and Peiyi gaped.

Madame Chang did not look like any woman Rendi had ever seen before. She was not like the painted ladies of the court, who giggled and swayed like flowers as the wind blew. Nor did she resemble a broad-shouldered peasant woman, thick and browned by the sun. Her features were fine and smooth, as if she had been carved from ivory, and the light in her dark eyes made them shine like stars. She stood with the elegance of a willow tree, and even though she wore the cotton robes of a commoner, both Rendi and Peiyi felt as if they should kowtow before her.

Peiyi's eyes were as large as lychees, and it took a moment before Rendi realized that they were both staring.

"Master Chao would like to know if you want all your meals brought to you in your room," Rendi said.

"It's cooler in the dining room," Peiyi said, and then with an attempt at a grown-up air, "but it's hot everywhere, these days."

"Yes, it is," Madame Chang agreed with a smile. "But at least it's not as hot as when there were six suns in the sky."

"Six suns?" Peiyi asked.

"You don't know the story?" Madame Chang asked, looking from Peiyi to Rendi. Both shook their heads.

THE STORY OF THE SIX SUNS

Long ago, so long that only the sky, mountains, and water can truly remember, six suns appeared in the sky. These six suns caused great suffering and devastation to the earth. Rain boiled away before ever touching the ground. The trees and plants withered, leaving behind only the scorched earth, burned and brown. All the villagers were forced to live like worms, crowding into an ancient dark hole in one of the hills. As they began to starve, they also began to despair.

But then a rumor began to murmur at night, perhaps sent by the Spirit of the Mountain above. "The one marked with power can save you," it whispered. "The one who bears the mark of power can save you."

The people looked at one another in confusion until a man stepped forward. His name was WangYi, and he was the strongest, bravest, and quickest of all men. He had already done many great deeds. They said he had tamed the flooding water serpent with just the fierceness of his eyes, and he had killed the single-toothed earth giant with his mighty strength. But more than that, WangYi had an unusual scar on his forehead. It looked like the character *wang*, a symbol of power.

"It must be WangYi whom the Spirit of the Mountain meant," the people said. "The scar is the mark of power!"

But when WangYi stepped on the scorched earth and gazed at the six suns, he knew his strength and fierceness would not help. He had to stand in the shade of the mountain, for the ground lit by the suns burned his feet. Everything on earth was suffering — even the giant tree next to the mountain seemed to be withering. WangYi realized that he could not fight the suns. His only hope was to shoot them down from the sky.

So he shot his arrows at the suns, pulling his mighty crescent bow so that it made the shape of a full moon. But no matter how powerfully he pulled, the arrows could not reach. Over and over he shot, until the shade of the mountain disappeared as the suns moved overhead. Finally, with only six arrows left in his case, WangYi was forced to dip his feet in water to cool them. He looked down in defeat.

It was then that he saw his reflection in the pool. The great lake had shrunk because of the heat, but the shade of the mountain had saved it from completely vanishing. There was still enough water for him to see the six suns reflected in it.

"I will shoot them here!" WangYi said. And with his back to the mountain, he quickly placed an arrow in his bow and shot at the reflection of one of the suns. As the arrow flew into the water, a sun sank from the sky. WangYi fitted another arrow and shot again. Another sun fell.

Immediately, the people felt a change in the temperature. They crawled out from the hole to watch WangYi shoot the third sun and then the fourth. But as everyone cheered, WangYi's wife thought quickly.

"If he shoots all the suns," she realized, "we will be forever in darkness."

So, knowing better than to disturb her husband's concentration, she crept behind WangYi as he prepared his arrow for the fifth sun. With all eyes on WangYi, only the mountain saw her as she silently took the sixth and last arrow from his case and swiftly hid it in her sleeve. As a result, after shooting the fifth sun, WangYi found his case empty and laid down his bow.

This is why there is now one sun.

"Well, that one sun is hot enough," Rendi said. The guest room had grown even hotter during the story, and a drop of sweat rolled down his forehead like a falling grain of rice.

"That is true," Madame Chang said, and she looked out the window at the dry, yellowing earth below. Then she looked again at Peiyi and Rendi. "Please tell Master Chao I will take the rest of my meals downstairs with the other guests. I think I would enjoy the company."

Rendi didn't think Madame Chang would much enjoy the company of old, slow-witted Mr. Shan, the inn's one regular mealtime guest, but he refrained from saying so. Instead, both he and Peiyi bowed respectfully and left the room.

CHAPTER

6

"You couldn't teach a pig how to snore!" Widow Yan snapped.

"I wouldn't have to," Master Chao roared. "I would just let it follow your example!"

In the garden, Rendi sighed. He was unsure which was worse, the sky's wailing at night or the screeching of Master Chao and Widow Yan during the day, for Master Chao and Widow Yan were fighting yet again. He did not know what caused the first argument between the two neighbors or when it had been, but every day was full of their quarrels.

Rendi returned to his weeding, though truly it was the snails he was tending. The inn's garden was not really a garden. It was a snail haven. As soon as a green shoot sprang from the dirt, snails covered it like a warty plague. Any surviving leaves were also ravaged, and the partially eaten greenery looked like delicate paper cuttings decorating the dark wall.

The only garden that was worse was the one on the other side of that wall. Snails also reveled in Widow Yan's garden. Their shells adorned her plants like brown berries. The only things more plentiful than Master Chao's and Widow Yan's snails were their insults to each other.

A door slammed, and Rendi saw MeiLan, Widow Yan's daughter, come out of the house next door, drooping like a magpie with a broken wing. That meant Peiyi was sure to come out and try to sneak a visit. Rendi knew Peiyi had formed a secret friendship with the older girl, admiring her like the mother and sisters she didn't have. MeiLan was pretty and gentle, with long hair tied up smoothly in a woven clasp and skin like a fresh peach. To little Peiyi, who went about constantly with bruised knees and tangled hair, MeiLan seemed a fine lady.

And sure enough, there was Peiyi now, taking advantage of her father's distraction, stealing out of the inn and over the low wall. *Perfect*, Rendi thought wickedly as the girls greeted each other. He began gathering snails and arranging them on the wall. When he was done, Peiyi would be so annoyed.

"Have you heard from Jiming?" MeiLan asked Peiyi.

"No," Peiyi said, her voice suddenly full of sorrow.

"Maybe he is too busy," MeiLan said with a sad sort of laugh. "Maybe he is in the city having a grand time, with a fine job and a wife."

"A wife?" Peiyi exclaimed. "No! Jiming couldn't get married that fast."

"One never knows," MeiLan said with a shrug.

"He wouldn't!" Peiyi almost shouted, and then she said in a soft voice that made Rendi's ears prickle, and he almost stopped organizing the snails, "He wouldn't have forgotten about you."

The older girl said nothing and looked off into the distance, as if searching for the end of the scorched, stone plain that stretched before them. Rendi continued to place the snails on the wall. So far, the snails just spelled out PEIYI.

"MeiLan," Peiyi said, "could you show me your wedding jewelry again?"

Peiyi's eager eyes made MeiLan smile. Like a flitting bird, she went into the house, returning with a dark red wooden box with vases of peonies painted on one side.

Sitting down, MeiLan carefully placed the box on her lap and, with an air of grand formality, threw back the lid. Peiyi squealed in excitement and pleasure. Rendi was pleased too, for now the snails were saying PEIYI IS A.

"This will be for my hair," MeiLan said, fastening a gilded metal comb ornamented with flowers made of pearls and jewels into Peiyi's hair. The ornaments sparkled with a hundred rainbows in the brilliant sun. MeiLan dangled glittering gold pieces. "These will be my earrings."

"Can I see that again too?" Peiyi said, pointing to an embroidered silk purse.

"Ah, my treasure of treasures," MeiLan said, taking it out carefully with grand reverence. "I will not get married without it."

It was a jade bracelet. As Rendi proudly finished arranging the snails, which now said PEIYI IS A MELONHEAD in bold characters on the wall, he looked up and saw MeiLan holding a simple, smooth circle of green without carvings or extra adornments. The vivid emerald-green color shone through to the edges of the bracelet and had a beauty and elegance that even the harsh sun could not cheapen. Rendi admired it more than MeiLan's ornate haircomb.

"Now, tell me the story too!" Peiyi begged.

What story? Rendi thought. How could there be a story about a bracelet?

"It is not much of a story," MeiLan said. "I don't know why you like to hear it so often."

"I just do," Peiyi said. "Please!"

MeiLan laughed, and Rendi, in spite of himself, listened.

THE STORY OF THE JADE BRACELET

hen I was about your age, my father became very ill. He knew he was dying, and one day he called me over to his bed and gave me this jade bracelet. It had been his

mother's and his grandmother's before that, and he had been keeping it for me. But now it was mine. "It's part of your wedding dowry," he said to me. "For when you get married someday. It's very, very valuable, so make sure you take good care of it."

Soon afterward, he died, and I began to wear the bracelet all the time. It was too big for me, and it was much too fine to wear every day, but I couldn't help it. It reminded me of my father, and seeing the glossy green circle on my arm made me feel like he was still with me. But my mother would yell at me. "You're going to lose it," she said. "Put it away someplace safe."

I didn't listen to her. Instead, I wore it all day and even to sleep, hiding it under my sleeve so she wouldn't see. But she was right. Because, one day, I did lose it.

I wasn't sure when or how, but when I realized it was gone, I felt as if my father had died again. I didn't say a word to my mother, who would have been horrified as well as angry, but just waited until nightfall to sneak out of the house to look for it.

Had I lost it when I was feeding the chickens? Or working in the garden? Or, horror of horrors, when I was getting water from the well? In the moonlight, I searched on my hands and knees throughout the yard, tears streaming down my cheeks. As the moon began to swim in the sky, I started to despair, and I could not help my sniffling.

"What's wrong with you?" a voice said.

It was the Chao boy — your brother, Jiming. He was sitting on the garden wall in the silver light of the moon and looking at me as if I were a curious animal. I knew I wasn't supposed to talk to him, because he was a Chao, but I didn't care. My misery overwhelmed my pride and anger. "I lost my bracelet," I almost wailed.

"Well, can you stop crying about it?" he said, and motioned to the inn where a loud howling echoed. "My baby sister has been crying and crying for hours, and I came out here to get away from it."

"I'll stop crying when I find my bracelet!" I said to him.

"Fine," he said, and he jumped from the wall. He got down next to me and started to help me look. "If it's the only way to get some peace here."

So we crawled in the grass, like two crickets in the

night. Neither of us said much, but even as we searched in silence, I was grateful he was there. I had always been told that the Chao boy and his family were awful, but right then, with the round moon glowing above, he didn't seem so bad.

And when Jiming found the bracelet next to the sleeping rooster, I knew he was not bad at all. "Is this it?" he asked, holding the bracelet in the air so that it mirrored the circle of the moon. I was so happy! I jumped up and hugged him, and then I laughed because he looked so surprised. As soon as the bracelet was in my hands, I ran inside to put it someplace safe — without even saying goodbye. But as I left, we both knew we were friends.

"I was a baby then," Peiyi said proudly. "My crying helped you and Jiming become friends."

"Yes," MeiLan said, "and we've been friends all these years, though we had to keep it secret from our parents."

"They probably wouldn't like us being friends either," Peiyi said.

"No," MeiLan said absently. She held the bracelet before her as if she could see her future through its hole. Softly, to herself, she repeated, "I will not get married without it."

"Peiyi!" Master Chao called from the inn. The fight with Widow Yan must have ended, for now the shouts were for Peiyi. "Where are you?"

Both girls looked up, alarmed. With haste, Peiyi removed the comb, and MeiLan put the bracelet back into its pouch and in her box. Then, scampering like a rabbit, Peiyi crossed over to the inn's yard, running past Rendi and the wall without a second glance.

Rendi stared. The wall was blank; his carefully arranged message of PEIYI IS A MELONHEAD was gone. For, without his noticing, the snails had slowly crawled back to the shelter of the shaded garden, leaving only a trail of ooze behind them.

CHAPTER

7

The sun was finally beginning to dip in the sky, and Widow Yan was frying her famous fermented tofu. It was strange how something that smelled so foul could taste so delicious. The joke about fermented tofu was that the more disgusting it smelled, the more delicious it was. Widow Yan's tofu seemed to be proof of this, as an odor reminiscent of rotting garbage mixed with an unemptied chamber pot reeked from it. Rendi could not think of anything that smelled more unpleasant, but he had often seen MeiLan sneak some of the tofu over the wall to Peiyi, who ate it with rapture.

Rendi brought the teacups to the table, setting them down one by one with a solid thud. With each thump, Master Chao groaned.

"Oh, my head!" Master Chao said, placing the palm of his hand to his forehead. "Please give me some quiet and some peace!"

Rendi grimaced. He needed peace more than Master Chao. Every day, he had to listen to the innkeeper's petty bickering, and at night the sky's crying tormented him. Rendi was starting to believe the sounds were all in his head. Was he going crazy? He tried not to think about it.

"I suppose one person's noise is another's friendly sound," Madame Chang said, turning to Mr. Shan at the table. "Much like the story of the rooster's cries to the sun, is it not?"

Mr. Shan started, jerked out of his thoughts for a moment. Rendi frowned and rolled his eyes. That afternoon, Rendi had watched when Madame Chang first saw old Mr. Shan, with his long white beard, hobbling on his cane through the door. She had gone straight to him, smiling, and took his hand into hers.

In return, Mr. Shan had stared at her vaguely as if seeing

her in a fog. Then he shook his head, sat down at his table, where his food was waiting, and immediately began chewing with an absentminded air. Rendi was surprised how graciously Madame Chang treated such a snub. Her smile waned, but instead of being insulted, her eyes softened, and she sat down next to him, pouring his tea. She had been kind and gentle to Mr. Shan, insisting on sitting with him at lunch, and now dinner, as if he were a beloved grandfather. Rendi couldn't understand it.

"Story?" Peiyi asked as she brought the teapot to the table. "Like this morning's story about the suns?"

"Yes," Madame Chang said to her, but she was looking quietly again at Mr. Shan. "Have the old stories been forgotten already?"

Mr. Shan stared back again in his confused way and said senselessly, "I lost the book."

Rendi swallowed an annoyed sigh. Mr. Shan was getting more witless every day.

"I want to hear it," Peiyi said. Rendi was eager as well, for there had been few tales told in the dull Inn of Clear Sky, but he flushed when he saw Madame Chang looking directly at him.

"Would you like to hear it?" she asked.

Rendi tried to shrug indifferently. "I guess so," he said.

THE STORY OF THE ROOSTER'S SONG

After WangYi shot down five of the six suns, the last sun fled from the sky. In fear, it hid inside a tall mountain.

Now, instead of boiling and burning, the people had another problem. The moon still floated in the sky, and its light made it possible for the villagers to see dimly, but it was not enough to warm the earth. The villagers huddled together as the plants and trees began to freeze.

"The sun must come out!" WangYi said.

Everyone agreed, but what could they do? They went to the mountain where the sun was hiding and threatened and pleaded and bribed to no avail. The sun refused to come out. But just as they began to despair, the wind murmured a message. "A friendly call will bring out the sun," the Spirit of the Mountain whispered. "A friendly call."

What did the Spirit of the Mountain mean? A friendly call? The villagers had tried sweet words and pleasant voices already, and the sun had not budged. It was WangYi's wife who understood.

"The sun does not consider us friends. It will not answer our call," she said. "We must find something that the sun thinks sounds friendly."

First they brought out the cricket, which had a pleasant chirp. But its sound was faint, and the sun could not hear it through the stone of the mountain.

So then they brought out the tiger, whose loud, angry roars echoed across the land. But the sound enraged the sun, and it spit fire in annoyance.

They decided, then, to bring out the cow. Its relaxed lows were sure to be calming to the sun. And they were. The sun, inside the mountain, was lulled by the cow's sound and almost went to sleep.

The villagers began to panic. "What sound will call

out the sun?" they asked themselves. "What will sound friendly to it?"

"Let us try the rooster," WangYi's wife said.

"The rooster?" the others said, dubious. Most found the rooster's voice to be grating and strident.

"It is loud enough to be heard through the stone," she said. "And its voice is not full of anger or leisure. Let us try the rooster."

So they brought out the rooster, which gave its loud, triumphant crow. The sun listened carefully. *What a nice noise*, it thought, and it peeked out of the mountain to see who was calling.

The sun's first rays reached out and touched the rooster. In its light, the rooster turned a radiant golden color with a comb as bright and as red as a burning flame. When the villagers saw this, they realized the sun was coming out, and they cheered as if it was a grand celebration. The sun, now hearing so many friendly sounds, was pleased, and it came all the way out of the mountain.

That is how the sun returned to the sky.

"But the rooster, the one that turned gold — was it special, then?" Peiyi asked.

"Yes," Madame Chang said, nodding. "It became the Celestial Rooster, and it is the sun's friendly companion to this day."

"And is this why the roosters crow in the morning?" Rendi couldn't help asking. He was thinking about Widow Yan's rooster, which woke him up every morning just as the night stopped its moaning and he was able to fall asleep. He disliked that rooster very much.

"Yes," Madame Chang said, giving him a pleased smile. "The roosters are calling out the sun, just like the Celestial Rooster did a long time ago."

"A long time ago," Mr. Shan echoed unexpectedly. For a moment, Rendi saw a flicker in his eyes, a sharp brightness he had never seen before. But then it disappeared, and Mr. Shan slurped from his bowl, dribbles of soup falling into his beard.

CHAPTER

8

At night, the sky remained moonless, and the mournful sounds, as much as he tried to ignore them, kept Rendi awake in his bed. He gritted his teeth in frustration. How many nights had the sky wailed? How long had he been in this village? Would a new guest ever come?

But a new guest had come. For a moment, Rendi stopped his usual glowering and started to think about Madame Chang. She had brought no cart for him to hide in, but she had brought stories. And when she told them, Rendi had felt transported—away from the village and inn he despised and from unwanted memories. He remembered Madame Chang looking at him with that pleased, almost tender smile. It had been a smile that a mother would give her child, and it filled Rendi with a longing that made him turn and sigh in his bed almost as much as the groaning sky.

"*Ooooooo-oooooohhh*." A muffled whine blended into the howls of the sky. But this moan had no eerie echo and came from right outside Rendi's room. He rose from his bed and opened the door to see Peiyi huddled in the doorway of her room across the way with a lantern.

"It's so dark," Peiyi said. "The stars don't really shine, and the moon is gone."

Did she hear the wails? Was it not just in his head? Rendi began to ask but then looked at Peiyi's small, upturned face. As her frightened eyes met his, he saw the start of tears forming. A wavering softness seemed to curl inside Rendi, like smoke from incense. Peiyi reminded him so much of . . . the memory stung him with a slapping pain. Rendi scowled.

"You probably just scared it away with your drippy pig nose," he said.

Fear disappeared from Peiyi's face as anger replaced it. "Horrible! You don't care about anything!" she said, her white cheeks turning red with rage. "Everyone else leaves. Why won't you?"

"Peiyi, why aren't you sleeping?" Master Chao's voice called from the stairs. As he came into view, Rendi felt himself flush. "And you too, Rendi?"

"We were just..." Rendi began, but Master Chao cut him short.

"Go to bed," Master Chao said. "Both of you."

They nodded, and Rendi silently retreated to his room. However, inside he was seething and wanted to scream with the sky. "Everyone else leaves. Why won't you?" Peiyi had said. He would leave if he could! If only a guest with a carriage or cart would come. It wouldn't matter where it was headed. Any place would be better than here! Any place but here, Rendi thought, or home.

But it was here he was stuck. The next morning brought the rooster's crow, the hot sun, and a new chore, but no new guests. Rendi sagged at the table at breakfast.

"That old well in the back dried up for good last week," Master Chao said. "And now it's falling apart. I don't want a guest taking a night stroll to fall into it. Rendi, you'd better fill it up this morning."

"Fill it?" Rendi asked.

"I guess it's the first well in the village to go dry," Master Chao said. "If something doesn't change, there'll be more. Pretty soon, all the villagers will have to get their water from the Half-Moon Well like we do. Peiyi will show you where the shovel is."

Moments later, with the shovel on his shoulder, Rendi followed Peiyi as she crossed the yard with skipping leaps. The sun seemed to be rising up into the sky by jumps and leaps as well because the top of Rendi's head felt as if it were smoldering. Full of resentment, he thought of shaded pavilions and cool, iced plum juice brought by bowing servants.

What am I doing here? Rendi glared in disgust as he slowly began to dig the crumbly earth. The ground was surprisingly soft and light and without any heavy rocks or stones. *More like dust than dirt*, Rendi thought. He looked across to the barren plain of stone left by the missing mountain. "I guess all the stone is there."

As Rendi dropped a shovelful of dirt into the well, it

seemed to scatter down like drops of water being shaken from a tree after the rain. But as the earth fell, a strange, deep sound began to echo. "*EERRR-rripp! EERRR-rripp!*" groaned the well.

"Rendi!" Peiyi said as she threw herself on the ground and peered into the deep hole. "There's something in there!"

CHAPTER
9

Rendi kneeled and looked into the hole. Peiyi was right. There was something there. In the blackness at the bottom, two beady eyes looked at him.

"*EERRR-rripp!*" it croaked up. Rendi almost laughed. It was a toad.

It was an old, ugly, warty toad, sitting on a rock in a dark puddle of water. The toad moaned again, reminding Rendi of the mournful sounds that kept him up at night. Was it this toad that had been making the wails in the sky? Impossible. Those sounds bellowed in his ears like loud thunder. This toad's croak was at most a faded echo.

"It's just a dumb old toad," Rendi said, and threw in another heap of dirt. The toad groaned again.

"Stop!" Peiyi said, jumping up. "You'll kill it!"

"I'm not killing it," Rendi said, irritated. "I'm filling the well. I'm doing what your father told me to do."

Rendi tossed in another pile of dirt, and "*EERRR-rripp! EERRR-rripp!*" the toad wailed, over and over again, as if now realizing what was happening. The cries were like the sounds of a funeral horn.

"Stop it! Stop it!" Peiyi screamed, grabbing his arm. "You'll bury it alive!"

"Who cares?" Rendi sneered, and pushed away Peiyi's hands. The sun was scorching his head and arms, and he was burning inside as well. He didn't care about anything in this hot, dried-up village. If he could, he would bury all of it! Everything! Anything to make his past, the crying night, and the Village of Clear Sky disappear.

"What is wrong?" Madame Chang said, her gentle voice blowing over him. As he and Peiyi turned around, Rendi again felt as if they should kowtow on the ground before her. She stood there gracefully, her dark eyes gazing down upon them, and Rendi felt ashamed.

"Rendi has to fill the old well, but there's a toad down there," Peiyi said in a pleading tone. "If he fills it, he'll kill the toad."

"I see," Madame Chang said. Careless of the fabric of her silver-gray robe, she kneeled beside the old well, looked in, and smiled. "Too hot for fur?" she said to the toad. Peiyi gave Rendi a confused look, and he shrugged.

The toad continued its melancholy song, and Rendi wondered what Madame Chang would do. The well was too deep for her to reach the toad, even with a stick. Would she ask him to get a rope and climb down? He cringed. The decrepit old well was cracking and breaking—it was likely that part of the well would collapse with him in it.

Suddenly, the toad was silent. Madame Chang stood up. "You can continue your work, Rendi," she said.

"But if he fills the well, the toad..." Peiyi sputtered, torn between her manners for a guest and her feelings.

"Don't worry," Madame Chang said, gently putting

her hand on Peiyi's shoulder and leading her away. "The toad will be fine."

Peiyi looked doubtful, but as she continued to look at Madame Chang, her expression slowly cleared and transformed into one of puppylike adoration. If Peiyi had admired pretty MeiLan as a lady, she was now worshipping Madame Chang like a queen. Rendi stared at their backs as they both walked away.

In silence, he shoveled earth into the well. Madame Chang's appearance had been like a soft wind cooling his anger, and now Rendi began to feel troubled. Each drop of earth weighed upon his conscience. Was he killing the old toad? Why was the well quiet? Had the toad found another way out? Or was it dead already? Finally, Rendi looked over the edge.

His mouth fell open. He couldn't believe what he saw. The toad was sitting cheerfully on a pile of dirt — the same dirt that Rendi was flinging into the well. Rendi tossed in another mound and then watched as the toad shook it off and vigorously jumped, patting the earth down into a surface. The toad was making a hill from the dirt that was filling the well. With each shovelful Rendi threw in, the toad rose higher.

So Rendi continued to dig. His hands were chafed raw, and he had been obliged to dig farther and farther away from the well in order to not create another hole. The sun made his head feel as if it were a burning blister, and sweat dripped from his brow like a melting icicle.

Finally, the toad was getting closer to the top of the well. Now Rendi could see it sitting attentively on the dirt pile, its brownish green warts making it look like a piece of rotten wood covered with mushrooms. The toad's black eyes were flashing in eagerness.

Just when it was high enough for the toad to see out of the well, it gathered itself like an expectant warrior. With one last shake, the ugly, ancient toad gave a bellowing croak, a war cry, and with a powerful leap, jumped onto solid ground next to Rendi's feet.

"*EERRR-rripp!*" the toad burped.

CHAPTER
10

The toad looked up at Rendi triumphantly, as if expecting applause. Rendi could only stare. The toad gave another burp, this one sounding a bit offended. It turned away from Rendi and began to gaze at the stone field. It sat listening to the light breeze, its neck strained forward as if a voice was calling to it. Rendi looked at the toad again. It seemed ordinary enough, mold-colored, fat, and lumpy. If anything, it was uglier than most toads. But Rendi had never seen a toad act like this.

Then, with a clumsy *Plop!* the toad jumped. *Hop! Plop!*

It began to make its way toward the Stone Pancake — it was easy to see that the toad meant to cross it. Rendi quickly moved.

"Don't go there, you dumb toad!" Rendi said, placing the shovel in front of its path. "It's miles of hot stone. You'll just get lost and cooked."

The toad made another insulted-sounding croak but looked again at Rendi as if reconsidering. Rendi felt curious and impressed at the same time. Then, as if a decision had been made, the toad turned around and hopped to the back door of the inn.

"*EERRR-rripp!*" the toad said loudly.

"Did you want to go in?" Rendi asked.

"*EERRR-rripp! EERRR-rripp!*" the toad said impatiently.

"It's lunchtime, anyway." Rendi shrugged and opened the door.

The toad began to hop into the inn. Rendi couldn't help following, matching his steps to the toad's jumps. Where was it going? He felt as if he were tied to the toad with an invisible thread.

The toad turned toward a room Rendi had never

entered before. "I don't think you should go in there, Toad," Rendi said. But the toad was not listening. He disappeared into the room, and Rendi, after hesitating a moment, followed.

It was a small, dark room, and the light from the doorway poured into it like spilled water. The harsh daylight was softened, diffused by the dusty ashes of incense floating in the air. It skimmed gently over the short, narrow table lined with incense holders and the row of gray slabs of stone that leaned against the wall. The stone tablets were carved with names of dead ancestors and blackened by smoke. This was the Chao family's shrine room.

The toad plopped before a tablet and gave a sad, mournful croak — again reminding Rendi of the sad cries he heard from the night sky. Rendi stepped closer and caught his breath as he read the name of Peiyi's mother. He hadn't really thought about Peiyi's mother until that moment, he realized, and a sudden guilt filled him. "Everyone leaves," Peiyi had said, and she had meant her mother as well. However, Peiyi's mother had not only left but was also never coming back. All that Peiyi saw of her mother now was a carved name on a cold, dark stone.

"EERRR-rripp!" the toad said. Rendi saw that the toad was leaving the room. He followed.

The toad turned into the hallway, leaping confidently. Rendi felt his amusement returning. *Hop! Plop! Hop! Plop!* Each jump gave a resolute thud, and the toad continued forward with a determined air. As they got closer to the dining room, Rendi could hear people talking.

"...He's always angry. He doesn't care about anyone except himself. He hasn't ever smiled or laughed or been nice since he's been here!" Peiyi was saying.

"Never smiled?" Madame Chang said thoughtfully. "He's too young to be that troubled."

Rendi realized they were talking about him and tried to retreat, but it was too late. *"EERRR-rripp! EERRR-rripp!"* the toad called loudly, announcing their presence. Everyone turned toward them, and Rendi froze in the entryway.

But no one was looking at Rendi. All eyes were on the toad. Despite Master Chao's look of horror, it was gleefully leaping across the floor, making croaking sounds like guffaws of laughter. With a last great joyful spring, the toad bounded into the air and onto Mr. Shan's ragged, unkempt lap.

CHAPTER

11

Rendi looked down at his rice. He wasn't sure if he was more surprised that he was sitting at a dining table reserved for guests or that Madame Chang was smiling. Because instead of being disgusted that a fat toad had landed next to her, Madame Chang had beamed as if greeting an old friend. Her welcome had included Rendi, who she had insisted sit with her, Mr. Shan, Peiyi, and the toad for lunch. Master Chao had shrugged permission, Madame Chang's choice of a chore boy as a dining companion as perplexing to him as her choice of the toad.

However, the toad's company seemed to be more appreciated than Rendi's. Peiyi clapped her hands, and Mr. Shan had brightened and smiled at it. Looking more awake and alive than Rendi had ever seen him before, Mr. Shan had petted the toad and then reached into his pocket and took out two copper coins tied together with a red string. He rattled it in front of the toad, like a toy in front of a baby. Instead of groaning painful sounds like the ones Rendi heard at night, the toad was now gurgling and giggling.

"You're playing with a toad," Rendi said with a note of disgust. Peiyi rolled her eyes. "It's more fun than you," she said.

He began to respond with a rude insult, but suddenly the image of the cold, grim stone tablet came into Rendi's mind. He closed his mouth.

"Rendi," Madame Chang said as he paused, "Peiyi says that you haven't ever smiled since you've been here. Is that true?"

Rendi shrugged.

"Yesterday, I noticed that you seemed to enjoy my story," Madame Chang said. "Am I right?"

Rendi nodded grudgingly. "It was interesting," he said.

"Well, I want to make a deal with you," Madame Chang said. "If I can make you smile...no, if I can make you laugh with this next story, then for every story I tell, you must tell one of your own."

"I don't know any stories!" Rendi protested.

"Oh, I'm sure you do," Madame Chang said, smiling at him in a teasing way. "You've just never shared them before. And I'll give you plenty of time to think of one — you can tell yours at dinner."

"I want to hear the funny story!" Peiyi said. Mr. Shan nodded, and the toad croaked as if in agreement. Even Master Chao, standing at the back of the room, seemed to be looking at Rendi.

Rendi shrugged again. "Does it have to be a good story?" he asked.

"Any story you want," Madame Chang said. "We won't complain."

"I will!" Peiyi said, but Madame Chang ignored her.

"Is it a deal?" Madame Chang said, looking at Rendi. He hesitated.

"Oh, Rendi!" Peiyi said, irritated. "You're not going to laugh anyway."

"All right," Rendi said. *Why not?* he thought.

Madame Chang smiled. Unexpectedly, she turned her head and looked at Master Chao. He had been pretending that their conversation was unworthy of his attention, but it was plain to see that he had been listening closely. He quickly looked away and pushed the beads on his abacus, as if he were deep in calculation. Madame Chang's smile grew larger, and she began the story.

THE STORY OF THE OLD SAGE

Once there was an old man who lived on a mountaintop. Some thought he was a crazy old man. Others thought he was the Mountain Spirit or even an immortal. But most believed he was a sage of great wisdom.

Many sought him — some for answers, some for

advice, and some to be his students. The old man answered all the questions and solved all the problems, but he shooed away all the hopeful students. However, one student named Tiwu refused to give up. He returned over and over again, begging and pleading, until finally the sage agreed to teach him.

Tiwu was an eager pupil. At the sun's first light, the sage would share the old stories and teachings, and they would spend the rest of the day in deep contemplation. But at night, when the moon climbed into the sky, the old man ignored his student and, instead, read to himself from a large book.

Tiwu wondered about this. It was obvious to him that there was great wisdom in the book that only the sage read. What special knowledge was in it? He yearned to know. But the sage never offered him even a glance at one of the pages.

However, Tiwu was a reasonable fellow. *He will allow me to read the book*, he thought, *when I have mastered everything else he has taught me.* So he set his mind on his lessons, learning in earnest.

And with such effort, his progress was quite

considerable. Soon, when people came to the old sage for answers, Tiwu was able to give them. Before long, Tiwu also began to gain the reputation of being a wise man.

Encouraged by this, Tiwu finally gathered the courage to ask the sage about the book. One night, as the old man read silently, Tiwu asked, "Master, what are you reading in that book?"

"The page I am reading right now," the old man said without looking up, "is about the secret to attaining peace."

The secret to peace! Tiwu was in awe. Only the wisest and greatest of sages would know that. The book was full of wonderful secrets! What other extraordinary answers were in that book?

"Master," Tiwu said, "may I read the secret to peace too?"

The old man looked at him. "Do you really wish to know the secret to peace?" he asked. "Or do you simply wish to read the Book of Fortune?"

Tiwu thought carefully and then said honestly, "Both."

The sage said nothing, stroking his beard in thought. Tiwu could sense his doubt. Finally, the sage said, "Do you really believe you are ready?"

"Yes," Tiwu said confidently. In his mind, the only thing that kept him and the sage from being equals was the knowledge in the book.

"I am not sure," the old man said.

"I am!" Tiwu said. "Please, how can I prove it to you?"

The sage sat thoughtfully for a moment and then said, "At the bottom of this mountain, you will see a tall tree overlooking a lake. Climb the tree to the highest branch and sit there in contemplation for ninety-nine days and nights. If you are able to do that, you may read the Book of Fortune and the secret to achieving peace."

Immediately, Tiwu traveled down the mountain, and he found the tall tree overlooking the lake. The tree was smooth and straight, like a giant paintbrush, and seemed almost as tall as the mountain he had just left. With great difficulty, Tiwu wrapped a rope around the trunk of the tree and made his way up to the highest branch.

At the top, he sat in complete confidence. He was sure he could meet his master's requirements and return to learn the great secret. The sun rose and dropped, the moon filled and emptied, and Tiwu watched it all from the top of the tree. Nearby villagers, finding it easier to call up questions to someone in a tree than to climb a mountain, sent him baskets of food, which he hauled up using his rope. Soon, he began to bestow answers and advice to a steady stream of followers.

On the ninety-sixth night, there was a terrible storm. The wind shrieked and screamed, and the thunder's roars echoed for miles away. Lightning slashed the sky, and rain attacked like vicious arrows. The tree swayed and bent, but Tiwu, remembering his master's teachings, did not panic. Even as nearby branches cracked and fell and rain and wind slapped his face raw, he sat silently, like a stone statue.

The next morning, everyone crowded around the tree to see Tiwu sitting calmly up in the branches. "He is, without a doubt, a great sage," they said to one another. "Only one who has achieved real enlightenment could be unmoved by that storm." And they hailed and honored him from the ground.

Tiwu heard their praises and felt quite satisfied. *I have truly proven myself*, he thought, and wrote a poem:

> *Like a mountain of stone,*
> *The most powerful wind,*
> *The most thunderous noise,*
> *Cannot move me.*
> *Steadfast my mind,*
> *Deliverance my gain.*

This he decided to send to his master, the old man on the mountain. One of Tiwu's admirers quickly brought it to the sage. The old man read the poem and smiled. Then he flipped the paper over and wrote in dark characters:

BURP

And sent it back to Tiwu.

Tiwu quickly read the reply, expecting praise from his teacher. When he saw what his master had scrawled on the page instead, Tiwu was very insulted. "'Burp'!" he said indignantly. "I speak of sacrifice and great knowledge, and he returns this? What does he mean?"

Offended, Tiwu rushed down the tree and up the mountain. With every step, he felt more resentful of his master's response. So when he finally saw the old sage sitting calmly, Tiwu immediately began to berate him. "What is this?" Tiwu said, waving the message angrily. "'Burp'! What did you mean?"

The old man waited until Tiwu paused for breath. "You said the most powerful wind and the loudest noise could not move you," the sage said with a smile. "But it took only one burp to bring you here."

With those words Madame Chang finished the story and looked at Rendi. His mouth had curved, and a noise snorted out of his nose. It was only when the sound joined everyone else's that he realized he was laughing.

CHAPTER

12

After lunch, Rendi went to collect water from the Half-Moon Well. Ever since he had arrived at the Village of Clear Sky, all his time from lunch until dinner was spent doing this. Rendi walked back and forth on the twisting street between the inn and the well, until the sun sat right on the horizon like a balancing egg yolk.

The Half-Moon Well was divided by a crumbling stone wall. It had been the wall of a courtyard, protecting a wealthy home when the Village of Clear Sky was rich and prospering. At that time, the owner must have been generous, for he had dug half the well beyond the wall so that poor peasants could use it too. To them, the split well had looked like the half circle of the midmonth moon, so they called it the Half-Moon Well. However, now, with the wall in ruins, the well looked more like a full moon with a scar down its center. Rendi cursed it daily.

The Half-Moon Well was an awkward shape to haul water from, the dividing wall making the openings too small for buckets. Rendi was forced to use a small hollow gourd to draw up the water, which he emptied into the large buckets he carried to and from the inn. Every day, Rendi had to gather enough water for the garden and the inn, and he often felt as if he were trying to fill a lake using a spoon.

Today, however, Rendi did not curse the well. He did not think of the wails in the sky that gave him no peace at night. He did not even plot or plan how he could leave the village. Instead, he was busy trying to think of a story to tell at dinner. He tried to remember old fairy tales told to him or to make one up, but his mind remained empty. "Why did I agree to tell a story?" he groaned to himself. "Why does she want me to tell a story, anyway?"

So while his head was empty, the rest of him was full of anxiety. Even as he filled the oversize buckets with the gourd, his thoughts were turning and twisting like dough deep-frying in oil.

Perhaps that was why, when Rendi had finished the tiring process of filling the buckets, he paid less attention to his feet than he should have. He had just balanced the carrying stick on his shoulders, still thinking furiously, and was stepping over the well, when his back foot caught on the partition wall. In that instant, Rendi tripped — his buckets swung madly like crazed pendulums, splashing water in large waves, until everything, including Rendi, crashed to the ground.

"Owww!" Rendi cried.

He lay facedown on the hard, dusty earth. Pain flashed through him, and a bump was already forming on the back of his head where one of the buckets had struck him. But it was anger that was burning through Rendi like a hot fire. Already, the spilled water — the water that took him so long to collect — was drying in the sun.

"Stupid, stupid wall!" Rendi roared, jumping up and kicking the partition with his foot, resulting in new stabs

of pain. With a yelp of anger, he began attacking the wall with all his strength.

Boiling rage seemed to have bubbled and burst inside him. His every muscle throbbed with red fury. The air seemed to shriek in his ears, and the fierceness of his anger felt like explosions inside his head. His pole cracked and the buckets bounced from the wall, but Rendi still felt as if he were ablaze with a thousand bee stings. He fell to his knees and grabbed a rock with each hand and raised them to strike.

But suddenly, his hands froze in the air and the rocks dropped to the ground.

For, unexpectedly, he saw his reflection in the well. The water on both sides of the well mirrored him, showing him in a way he had never seen before — roaring with anger and filled with rage.

"I look like . . . I look like . . ." Rendi gasped, "my father!" He felt as if a searing knife had been stabbed into him, the reflections in the water revealing a likeness he almost could not bear. For a moment, he was blinded by a mix of memories, pain, and regret.

When his vision cleared, Rendi was staring again at

two images of himself. The faces that looked back at him were troubled and uneasy. He felt tired, as if he had been running for days. Tears stung his eyes. But the water and the stones of the wall were as still and unmoved as if they were the empty sky above.

CHAPTER 13

During dinner, Rendi could sense everyone waiting for him. He had been late, for not only had he had to refill his buckets, they had also sprung leaks from his abuse, and he had to carry them by hand, as he had broken his pole. So when he finally entered the inn, the expectant eyes weighed upon him even more than the thick, sticky summer air.

Mr. Shan and the toad both croaked eagerly, and Master Chao was unusually attentive while Rendi picked at the rice in his bowl. The thick dark bowl, the color of burned wood, weighed heavily in Rendi's hands as he tried to avoid looking at Madame Chang.

She said nothing, letting him push the grains of rice with his chopsticks and chew air long after everyone else had finished their meal. The sky darkened and grew heavier and heavier. Rendi cringed inside. The night would soon begin its crying, which would not help him with his storytelling. Perhaps he could make an excuse or pretend... Peiyi gave an impatient sigh.

"Come on, Rendi!" Peiyi said. "Stop trying to think of a trick to get out of telling a story."

"I'm sure Rendi is still just thinking of what he wants to tell," Madame Chang said. "Whenever you are ready, Rendi."

Rendi flushed at the truth of Peiyi's words. Madame Chang's kindness made him feel ashamed, but, suddenly, as if by magic, "I have a story to tell," Rendi said.

"Really?" Peiyi said in disbelief.

"Yes," Rendi said, and began.

THE STORY OF THE DANCING FISH

Once there was a powerful magistrate. Even though his son and daughter were not supposed to have heard, they knew that everyone called their father Magistrate Tiger. It was a fitting name, for the magistrate always seemed to be roaring — at his servants, his wife, and even his children. And whenever he roared, all jumped to do his bidding.

"The blood of the greatest ruler and hero pumps in us!" Magistrate Tiger would thunder to his young children, the green silk of his sleeves flapping. "We must make the world bow to us again!"

Of course, Magistrate Tiger's children did not know what their father meant, and they were, in fact, too frightened to ask. But they knew that their father was always working to become more powerful and that he even hoped the emperor himself would acknowledge him. Often, Magistrate Tiger made trips out of his district, trying to get closer and closer to being accepted by the imperial family. His children never knew if he was successful, but they did enjoy his frequent absences — the sight of a waiting carriage made his son feel like a bird about to take flight.

The only people Magistrate Tiger did not roar at were his superiors. To kings and dukes and princes, his voice was silky and smooth. But perhaps they still would have called him Magistrate Tiger — to them, he purred like a cat.

And he did more than purr, his son found out. One day, Magistrate Tiger arrived home with an expensive qin. Magistrate Tiger had never shown interest in music before, so the entire household was surprised to see the stringed instrument in his hands — and they were even more shocked when Magistrate Tiger began to teach himself how to play.

After mastering a few simple songs, Magistrate Tiger called his children to him. Wearing a robe of brilliant green, he gave each of them a bowl of rice and, carrying the qin, had them follow him into the garden.

They stopped in front of the pond, where dozens of

bright orange carp waved in the water. Magistrate Tiger stationed his children on either side of him and, as he began to play the qin, instructed them to throw rice out into the water. The fish, seeing the food, began to jump up to eat the rice.

Every day they did this. As Magistrate Tiger played the qin, the children threw rice and the fish rushed for the food. Magistrate Tiger urged the children to throw the rice higher and higher, and the fish began to leap from the water to catch the grains. The children laughed and it was, the son thought, the most enjoyable time he had ever spent with his father.

But one day, when the son was playing up in a tree next to the pavilion of the fishpond, he saw his father, wearing his customary green silk robe, walking with his qin and a strange man. The man walked as if his neck could not bend toward the earth, and, judging from the fineness of his clothes, he could only be a grand official or some sort of royalty. The son, who was not supposed to climb trees in the garden, quickly found a branch that hid him from view.

"Ah, Duke Zhe," Magistrate Tiger was saying in his

smoothest voice, "I am so honored that you have finally accepted my invitation to visit."

"When I heard you are a connoisseur of music, I felt obliged to come," the duke said.

"Did you?" Magistrate Tiger said in surprise.

"Yes," Duke Zhe said. "Music reveals much about a person's character, does it not? Emotions and thoughts are communicated by it."

"Oh, yes," Magistrate Tiger said, nodding. "I've heard you follow the ancient philosophy of music."

"I suppose I do." Duke Zhe smiled. "And not just music but sound itself. If a listener truly understands, he can hear what others cannot. Sentiment and sound cannot be separated."

"I've often thought the same," Magistrate Tiger said, and stood by the fishpond as if in deep thought.

"Ah, but I'm not here to spout philosophy," Duke Zhe said. "I'm here to hear you play! The finer the music, the more noble the person — is that not true?"

"My playing is elementary," Magistrate Tiger said humbly. "But I do try to convey my most noble thoughts with it."

And without any further words, Magistrate Tiger began to strum the qin. As his familiar chords rang through the air, the fish began to jump out of the water, expecting the rice that had always been there before. They leaped again and again, as if dancing to the music. They shimmered in the sunlight, soaring and diving like cascades of orange and gold rainbows. It was beautiful.

Slowly, Magistrate Tiger stopped playing. The carp slowly stopped jumping. As the qin rested silently, the pond was calm. Duke Zhe looked amazed and, without a word, bowed to Magistrate Tiger.

"I have never experienced such a wondrous sight," Duke Zhe said. "To my ears, your playing was simple, but it must have conveyed such harmonious thoughts that only the fish could hear and rejoice at. You must be a very virtuous and wise man, Magistrate."

"Oh, you flatter me," Magistrate Tiger purred. "I simply try my best."

"Your name has come up once or twice at some of the imperial functions," Duke Zhe continued. "I will make sure that you begin to receive the attention you deserve."

"Thank you, Lord Duke," Magistrate Tiger said. "You are most gracious."

The duke turned around and began to walk back to the house. Magistrate Tiger moved to follow him, but before he turned, a look of triumphant conceit flashed on his face. The boy felt a shock run through him. It had been a trick!

His father had planned the whole thing, the son realized. The practicing at the pond, the throwing of the rice every day — they had been training the fish to jump to Magistrate Tiger's music. And all of it had been done just to influence Duke Zhe.

As Magistrate Tiger and Duke Zhe disappeared into the house, the boy dropped from the tree and stared blankly into the fishpond. It was clever of his father to trick the duke, was it not? But as he remembered Duke Zhe's serious, sincere face filled with awe, the boy saw his own face in the still water before him. And his own face looked guilty.

As Rendi finished the story, he looked at all of them staring at him silently. "You said it didn't have to be a good story," he said crossly.

"No, it was very good," Madame Chang said. "It was extremely interesting."

"Yes." Peiyi nodded. "I'm just surprised."

At that, Rendi grinned. And then he was the one who was surprised, because everyone smiled back.

CHAPTER

14

When Rendi finished his story, the sunlight had all but disappeared, and the night sky seemed to be swallowing the small inn. Even as Master Chao lit the large lantern in the open doorway, the blackness spread like spilled ink.

"So dark," Mr. Shan said, to no one.

After telling his story, Rendi felt surprisingly talkative, and the thoughts he had been holding inside began to leak out.

"It's because the moon is gone. It's missing," Rendi said.

"And the sky..." Rendi stopped. Did he dare mention the crying sky? Would they think he was crazy?

"Nonsense," Master Chao said. "Missing moon! It's just another moonless night."

"Rendi's right," Peiyi said. "The moon is lost."

"Well, we didn't lose it," Master Chao said. "Someone else can go find it. We have other things to do."

Rendi swallowed his disappointment. No one cared about the moon, and the wails he heard in the night probably were just in his head. As if agreeing, the dark sky began to sigh—a sad, miserable whimper. When Rendi looked up, Madame Chang was standing in front of him, looking out the window. There was a sadness in her eyes that he did not understand.

"It is better to light a lantern than to bemoan the darkness," Madame Chang said softly to herself, as if in a dream.

Peiyi heard her. "Can't we light more lanterns, then?" she said eagerly. "To make up for the light of the moon?"

"More lanterns?" Master Chao said, and a worried look flashed over his face. He stroked the red cinnabar beads of his belt decoration the same way he touched the beads of his abacus, and suddenly Rendi saw that Master Chao had much more pride than he did wealth. "Peiyi, it would just be a waste of lantern oil."

Madame Chang slowly turned. "We can't make up for the light of the moon," she said to Peiyi. "But we can make some light without wasting oil."

She walked out through the door, as graceful as a curving wisp of gray smoke. Rendi and the others watched, silently captive, as she plucked a handful of tall, dry grass from the front of the inn. Her silver outline seemed to glide against the sky, making her look like a night fairy. And when she lit the ends of the grass with a small flame, Rendi, Peiyi, Mr. Shan, and Master Chao drew around her like moths.

She smiled at them, holding the sheafs of lit grass as if they were incense sticks. The tips of the grass were burning orange embers, like bright seeds of light illuminating her face. Then Madame Chang waved her arm, and the embers glittered and scattered and flew in the darkness — a thousand tiny, glinting diamonds against the black silk of the night.

Madame Chang pulled a delicate, thin cloth from her

neck. With a swift motion, the sheer fabric billowed over the flashing sparks as if capturing them in a diaphanous cloud.

Indeed, they were captured, for after Madame Chang knotted the cloth, she was holding a soft, glowing bag of light. Rendi, Peiyi, Mr. Shan, and Master Chao stood with a mix of fright and amazement. What magic had Madame Chang done? Madame Chang handed the bag to Peiyi, who took it with hesitation.

Peiyi looked closely, and her face transformed from timidity to joyful wonder. "Fireflies!" she whispered, enchanted. "It's a firefly lantern!"

The others crowded around, all fear disappearing. The bag was full of fireflies, and when Rendi looked up, there were hundreds and hundreds more — somehow summoned by Madame Chang. They were flickering and twinkling all around them, and Rendi felt as if he were in the Starry River of the Sky.

Mr. Shan whooped like an excited young boy. "Firefly lanterns!" he hooted. "You can read under this light too!"

With more energy and quickness than Rendi had ever

imagined he had, Mr. Shan dropped his walking stick and leaped across the yard, his long legs making him look like a prancing deer. His beard flapped behind him as he tried to catch fireflies with his sleeve.

"Come on, Rendi!" Peiyi said, giving the firefly lantern to her father to hang. "There are enough fireflies to make lanterns for the whole inn!"

Rendi couldn't resist. Soon he found himself laughing a second time as he and Peiyi ran alongside Mr. Shan, collecting fireflies. Madame Chang supplied translucent cloth and paper for the gatherers, and Master Chao strung the lanterns on a line. The other villagers, attracted by the lights and noise, came out of their homes and were urged to join in by Peiyi and Mr. Shan. Soon, everyone in the whole small Village of Clear Sky was catching fireflies in front of the inn, enjoying themselves in a way they had not for a long time. Their faces were as radiant from pleasure as they were from the brightness, and even Widow Yan and MeiLan, unnoticed by Master Chao, gazed over the wall with smiles.

However, just as Madame Chang was handing Rendi another cloth, the sky gave a loud, plaintive wail, echoing

as if annoyed at being ignored. Rendi clutched his ears like he always did.

"Rendi," Madame Chang asked, shaking him gently, "what's wrong?"

"The night is crying!" Rendi said, unable to stop himself. "Don't you hear it? It's so loud!"

But Widow Yan, MeiLan, and the yard full of galloping villagers looked undisturbed, and Peiyi continued handing her father lanterns, obviously only hearing the sound of laughter. Mr. Shan was gazing at his bag of fireflies as if mesmerized. Had he heard it? Madame Chang looked at Rendi and stood very still. The wind moaned again.

"You don't hear it?" Rendi asked, almost begging. Was he imagining it? He didn't want to be crazy. "Peiyi and Master Chao and the villagers don't hear it either! What's wrong with me?"

"I hear it, Rendi," Madame Chang said, putting her hand on his shoulder to reassure him. "But I hear it only faintly. There's nothing wrong with you. You just hear it the most out of everyone."

"Why?" Rendi asked. "Why me?"

The sky sent out another pitiful groan, and Rendi looked at her in confusion.

"Remember your story?" Madame Chang said. "The duke believed that if a listener truly understands, he can hear what others cannot. You must understand in a way none of us do."

"But that wasn't true," Rendi protested. "The duke was tricked."

"The duke *was* tricked," Madame Chang said. "But that does not mean what he believed was false."

The light of the firefly lanterns flickered, and shadows wavered over Rendi's frowning face. At least he wasn't crazy, he thought. Rendi looked up at Madame Chang, and a hundred questions formed on his lips. But when the wind gave another restless whimper, Rendi asked, "Did Tiwu ever find out the secret to peace?"

Madame Chang pressed her hand softly on Rendi's shoulder and smiled. "What do you think?" she said.

Then she turned and left Rendi alone with his thoughts.

CHAPTER
15

"No moon, no rain, no rest," Rendi groaned to himself. Even though he was relieved that the night moans were not his imaginings, they still kept him up at night, making his sleep restless and poor. Peace could not be found in the daytime either. The sun baked the earth like a kiln, and Rendi felt like a hardened pot as he did his chores in the scalding sun. His frustration returned, and he again counted his days in the village with annoyance.

But when he watched Madame Chang come down the stairs for lunch, Rendi suddenly thought, *How stupid I've been! Madame Chang came by foot. I don't need to wait for a guest with a cart. I can just pack up my things and leave!* Rendi almost laughed out loud, his mood lightening. *Today,* he thought. *Maybe I'll go today.*

The others were in good spirits too, even the toad sitting next to Mr. Shan's lunchtime bowl of rice. The toad's wide mouth curved into something like a grin as Mr. Shan jangled the string of copper coins. The toad jumped as Mr. Shan jerked the coins, their clinking noises sounding like tiny bells. "Rabbit!" he said playfully to the toad. "Rabbit!"

"It's not a rabbit. It's a toad," Rendi said. Poor Mr. Shan, always confused.

"Ah, but it jumps like a rabbit," Mr. Shan said, looking at Rendi. Mr. Shan's gaze was disconcerting to Rendi, who realized he had never looked directly into Mr. Shan's eyes before. They were dark and deep, like the inside of the well Rendi gathered water from. But the expression in them was slightly lost, as if he were being led by a faint, faraway lantern.

"And maybe it is a rabbit inside," Madame Chang said. "Even when WangYi's wife was transformed into a toad, she was still herself inside."

"WangYi's wife?" Peiyi said. "Like in your story? The wife of the man who shot down the suns?"

Madame Chang nodded, and Peiyi seemed to bask in her glow. "Tell me," Peiyi begged.

"That depends on Rendi," Madame Chang said, looking at him. "If I tell another story, so must he."

Rendi flushed, and it was not from the heat. He felt everyone's eyes upon him again, and he shrugged. "It's fine," he said. What did it matter? he thought. He would be gone before he had to tell another story, anyway.

Madame Chang beamed and began the story.

THE STORY OF WANGYI'S WIFE

After WangYi shot down the suns, all hailed him as a great hero. The sky, earth, and seas echoed with his praises, and the people gave him every honor imaginable, including proclaiming him emperor.

But there was an even greater reward given to him. The Queen Mother of the Heavens, impressed by WangYi's deeds, requested a visit. When WangYi arrived at the Heavenly Palace, he was awed by its golden splendor and gave the Queen Mother his greatest respect and reverence. Well pleased by WangYi's humble deference, the Queen Mother decided to give him an unimaginable gift. It was a pill of immortality.

"It is not ripe yet," the Queen Mother told him when he opened the intricately carved box made from a golden peach pit. Inside was a slippery, round object — rather like a large frog's egg.

"Right now it is soft and clear," the Queen Mother continued. "But it will turn hard as jade and then white like the moon, until finally it will become gold like the sun. When the pill is gold, it is ready, and if you swallow it then, you will never die; you will achieve immortality."

Scarcely believing his good fortune, WangYi thanked the Queen Mother profusely and returned to earth. He hid the pill in his arrow case and told only his wife of its existence.

Then WangYi began to rule the people of the land. But gradually, as years passed, he became spoiled by all the admiration and glory. Slowly, he began to see everyone as his slaves and servants, existing only to do his bidding. Knowing that immortality waited for him, WangYi finally believed he should be treated as a god. He became proud and hard, demanding that his every whim be satisfied. He brutally punished anyone who displeased him, without more thought than if they were ants waiting to be crushed.

And through all this, WangYi's wife watched, grief-stricken, as the husband she loved changed into a cruel and selfish ruler. Again and again, she would plead for the punished and try to calm WangYi's arrogant anger. But before long, he did not even hear her gentle words.

Oh, how wretched her life became! How she despaired and wept! The shining gold of the palace could not brighten her misery, and her heart was heavy even as she wore delicate silk as fine as cobwebs. She shut herself in her rooms, unable to bear the sufferings WangYi was causing.

One late afternoon, in her unhappiness, WangYi's wife took out the poor cotton robes she had worn before WangYi had been made emperor. As her tears fell, she found the arrow that she had taken from WangYi's case, so long ago when he had shot down the live suns. Quietly, she went to return the arrow to the case.

But as she placed the arrow back, something seemed to flash at her like a flame. It was the golden box.

Almost immediately, she knew what it was. What else could be in such a wondrous golden box — carved with nine chrysanthemum flowers and gleaming in such a way that it could only be made from the pit of a peach of longevity? With trembling hands, she opened the box and stared at the white and glowing pill of immortality.

She could almost feel the power of the pill vibrating in her hands. *If WangYi becomes immortal*, she thought, *he will be emperor for all eternity.* She shuddered as she thought of him now, vain and pitiless. The pill was his and it did not belong to her, yet if he kept it his cruelty would continue forever. He would never forgive her, but "I can't let him take the pill!" she cried.

She threw the pill on the ground and stepped on it. She pounded it with a jade vase. She thrust it in a bowl of water. But the pill remained unharmed, smooth, and radiant like a lustrous pearl. It could not be destroyed.

And it could not be hidden safely either, WangYi's wife realized. If she hid it, he would search and search until it was found, not caring whom or what he destroyed until he got what he wanted.

Night had fallen, and she heard the heavy footsteps of WangYi coming for her. She fluttered around the room like a trapped butterfly, but as the clear light of the pill shimmered, she suddenly knew what to do. So when WangYi opened the door, she stood waiting for him with the shining pill in her hand.

He stared at her, surprised and speechless. And in that moment of shock, she put the white pill in her mouth and swallowed.

A searing pain swelled inside her as if she was being filled with a vicious poison. Her skin tightened, choking her, and her eyes closed as she fell to the floor, gasping. As she put her hands on the floor to lift herself, she was horrified to see that they had become mottled, wrinkled…and webbed! They were the hands of a toad!

When she looked up at WangYi, through his look of revulsion and fear, she could see her reflection in his eyes. It was not just her hands that were toadlike — she herself had been transformed into a giant toad.

WangYi, finally recovering from his astonishment, gave a shout of anger and started toward her. In terror, she jumped out the door and into the courtyard and the cool night air. As WangYi chased her, she leaped away with all her strength.

To the surprise of them both, her jumps brought her deep into the sky — higher than the palace rooftops and the mountain peak — into where the sky turned into the Starry River. The stars glittered around her like fireflies, and the night water clasped her with welcoming waves, but she was too frightened to understand what had happened. She could still hear WangYi's cries of fury, and her transformation into a toad had confused her.

In the distance, in front of her, she saw a round, glowing object as smooth and as white as a pearl. *Another pill!* she thought, bewildered. *I'll swallow that one too.*

She jumped toward it, her silhouette darkening its surface. But instead of swallowing it, she landed on it. For it was the moon, and her new home.

"But even as a toad," Madame Chang finished, "she was still herself on the inside. The pill she had swallowed just transformed her appearance."

"Did she always stay a toad?" Peiyi asked, wide-eyed.

Madame Chang smiled faintly. The sadness that Rendi had seen earlier in her eyes returned, and he looked at her curiously. "Many believe that as WangYi's wife lived on the moon, the pill slowly ripened inside her," she said. "And one day, when it was finally gold, she changed back into a woman and became the Moon Lady."

"The Moon Lady?" Rendi asked. He vaguely remembered hearing that name before and had a sudden vision of his mother tilting her head toward the moon with her eyes closed. "Doesn't the Moon Lady make wishes come true or something?"

"They say the Moon Lady can hear your most secret wish and grant it," Madame Chang said. "It may be a wish so secret that you don't even know you have it."

"Is your secret wish to turn back into a rabbit?" Mr. Shan said playfully to the toad, the coins tinkling as he rattled them. "You'll have to go to the moon!"

But there is no moon now, Rendi thought. *Without it, can the Moon Lady still grant wishes? Does she wish the sky would stop crying and the moon would come back? Would she grant my wish of leaving the Village of Clear Sky?*

CHAPTER
16

Rendi walked down the shady side of a twisted street; even the scant protection of shadows was welcome in the searing sun. *I'll just get some water at the Half-Moon Well, and then I'll pack up my things at the inn and leave,* he thought. The swinging sound of his mended buckets on his new carrying stick echoed against the crumbling stones of the empty ruins.

However, the ruins were not completely empty. In front of him, Rendi saw a figure at the Half-Moon Well. As he drew closer, he recognized Mr. Shan. He was on his knees, gazing into the well.

"Mr. Shan?" Rendi said, putting his buckets down. "What are you doing here?"

Mr. Shan did not seem to hear him and continued to look into the well. Rendi saw the toad, also at the well's edge, its bulging eyes gazing into the hole. Rendi kneeled by them and tried to see what they were looking at. All he saw was darkness and the slight shimmer of light on the deep water.

"Is something wrong with the Half-Moon Well?" Rendi asked.

"Half moon, it was not a half moon," Mr. Shan mumbled, as if he hadn't heard. "It was a full moon. I need a full moon to see."

And still without looking at Rendi, Mr. Shan put his hands on the wall that split the well in half and pushed down with a surprising force. *Crack! Crack!* The remains of the dividing wall crumbled and fell. Dry dust misted up into the air like steam, and the splashing noises of rocks falling filled the air. When all was quiet, the well was a round circle.

Rendi's mouth was also a round circle. He had struck that same wall with all his might, cracking his stick and breaking his buckets. All his efforts had not even loosened a single stone, yet Mr. Shan had knocked it down with a single push of his wrinkled, aged hands.

But Mr. Shan did not seem to be aware that he had done anything extraordinary. He peered again into the well. The reflections on the dark water sparkled up beams of light. The toad croaked a groan.

"Did you drop something down there?" Rendi asked after taking a deep breath and hiding his surprise.

"No, it's not in this water," Mr. Shan said, his eyes clouding over. "It's in a different water."

He's confused again, Rendi thought, and before he could be annoyed, he remembered Madame Chang's patient smile. "Mr. Shan," Rendi said, more gently than he ever had before, "I don't think there's anything in there."

Mr. Shan put the toad in his pocket and pushed himself up with his walking stick. "Yes, now there's nothing," he said, nodding in his absentminded way. "Don't jump in."

"Don't worry," Rendi said, amused. "I won't."

Mr. Shan's eyes seemed to clear, and he peered at Rendi,

the power of his gaze hitting Rendi like a falling stone. Rendi's smile faded, and a strange, discomforting feeling came over him, as if he had walked into a gray, clammy mist.

"Good," Mr. Shan said, nodding. He gently patted Rendi's shoulder. "Make sure you do as you say." And then Mr. Shan turned away.

Rendi stared at Mr. Shan slowly shuffling away, looking as ancient and as feeble as he always did. Rendi looked back at the well. A cold, icy wind seemed to blow through him. Suddenly, he had a vision of someone, something — a dark green blur — leaping into the gaping hole of the well, angry roars echoing upward. Rendi shivered.

Then he shook himself. The hot summer sun shone down, and its bright yellow light burned away any imaginings. He began to gather the water, which, now, with the partition gone, he was able to do faster than he ever had before.

However, when Rendi returned to his room at the inn, he still felt the weight of Mr. Shan's words. *Make sure you do as you say.* Rendi had said that he would tell a story for Madame Chang. They had an agreement. If he left now, he would be a liar and a cheater. *Like my father,* Rendi thought, and the sinking sun cast a dark shadow on his face.

Finally, he opened his drawers and took out his belongings, carefully folding them into his plain cloth bag. His last item was a smooth, blue-and-white rice bowl. It was thin and delicate, with faint traces of gold paint and a fineness that stood out in the poorness of his surroundings. Cupping it in his hands, Rendi gazed silently for a long moment.

"Why not?" he said.

CHAPTER
17

Rendi set down the chopsticks and the rice bowl, the thick, dark pottery of the bowl making a dull thud. While he waited for everyone else to finish dinner, he tried to look unconcerned and relaxed, even though he felt unexpectedly eager. He was pleased with himself. Tomorrow he would leave. But today he would do as he said he would and tell a story. It was better, anyway, Rendi thought. He wouldn't want to walk at night with the wind crying and moaning above him.

"Hmm," Peiyi said, looking at him from the corner of

her eyes. "Rendi, it almost seems like you want to tell a story."

Rendi looked away as if he'd been caught stealing. He quickly sipped his empty teacup, trying to look nonchalant.

"If you are ready," Madame Chang said, smiling, "we are willing to listen."

Mr. Shan and the toad seemed to nod in unison, and even Master Chao, giving up on his feigned indifference, looked up with interest. Rendi put down his cup and smiled in spite of himself. Then he took a deep breath and began his story.

 # THE STORY OF THE THREE QUESTIONS

Duke Zhe did as he promised. He spoke of Magistrate Tiger to the imperial family with glowing words, and before long, Magistrate Tiger's dreams began to come true. As the summer was ending, he received an invitation that was awe-inspiring. It was from the Imperial Palace and invited him to come to the emperor's Mid-Autumn Moon Festivities.

From that moment, Magistrate Tiger's home became a hectic typhoon. Magistrate Tiger's demanding roars echoed without stop as a new green robe was made and embroidered; costly gifts, sculptures of jade and gold, were inspected; and fine horses were groomed. Everyone and everything was so full of activity that it was with great surprise to the children when one day their father called them.

"Children are supposed to be good at riddles," he said as they bowed at his feet. "If you have any intelligence at all, you will know the answers to these."

The children stared silently at their father and gulped. Magistrate Tiger looked at their fearful faces and made an expression of disdain, as if he had just eaten an unripe plum.

"Here is the first question," Magistrate Tiger said. "A thief steals a purse and a man chases and catches him. However, when the authorities arrive, both men accuse the other of being the thief. Both men are of the same build and height, and bystanders cannot say for certain which is the thief and which is the pursuer. How can you tell?"

After a moment, just as Magistrate Tiger was about to sigh with impatience, the boy stepped forward.

"I would have the two men race," the boy said, trying to keep his voice from quavering, "and the loser is the thief. For if the pursuer was able to catch the thief, he must be the faster runner of the two."

Magistrate Tiger looked at his son keenly and then nodded. "Good," he said, and before the children could feel relief or pride, he continued.

"This is the second question," Magistrate Tiger said. "A single almond is given to a family of ninety-nine members. How can you share the almond evenly?"

The boy gave his sister a furtive glance, but she was already stepping forward with bright eyes.

"I would boil the almond in water and make it into almond tea," she said, "and then all can have a cup."

Magistrate Tiger sniffed in a satisfied manner. "The last question," he announced. "A pestilence of snails has come to a village. One man decides that the best way to get rid of the snails in his garden is to throw the snails into his neighbor's garden. Unfortunately, the neighbor has had the same idea, and snails begin to multiply in both gardens. Before long, the two families are fighting. How do you settle the dispute fairly?"

There was a long silence. Both children looked helplessly at each other. Neither had any idea of an answer. Finally, their father looked at them with disgust. "I see you are as feebleminded as I feared," he said with a scorn that stung more than a blow. His voice began to rise as his customary roar emerged. He threw up his arms, the green silk of his sleeves whipping at them. "You are a disgrace to our ancestry! The blood of the greatest ruler and hero pumps in us, and you cannot answer a simple question? Out! Out of my sight!"

The children fled and soon found themselves, as they often did, clinging to their mother for comfort.

"Why is he angry all the time?" the boy asked. Even though his sister was a year older than he, she was smaller and he often felt protective of her. He could feel her trembling like a baby rabbit, and he put his hand on her arm.

"He is not angry," their mother said unconvincingly. "It is just the way he must act to accomplish things."

"Why?" the boy asked, scowling. "For what?"

Their mother was quiet for a moment. "For you," she said finally. "He does all this for you."

The boy did not understand this either. But both children were glad that their father soon seemed to forget about them. Indeed, as the days came closer to the Mid-Autumn Moon Festivities, Magistrate Tiger seemed like a powerful storm that was best kept away from. When he finally left for the Imperial Palace, his children sighed with relief.

But the children were curious when Magistrate Tiger returned with an extra litter carried by strong men. The sedan they dragged did not hold a person, but a giant, well-wrapped package. Magistrate Tiger himself was carrying a silk box as if it were a dragon's pearl. The children looked at each other, then ran so they could peek in through the window of their father's formal chamber.

As the men carefully unloaded the package, Duke Zhe arrived.

"Ah, friend," Duke Zhe said warmly. "How happy I am for you! The emperor was much impressed by your wisdom and intelligence. Are these your prizes?"

"Yes, yes," Magistrate Tiger purred. "This is what the emperor gave me for answering the first question correctly."

And he opened the silk box and took out a blue, white, and gold rice bowl on a gold stand. He held it with an air of awe, and Duke Zhe gave a sigh of appreciation.

"Ah, the finest porcelain in the land, brought out especially for the emperor's Moon Festivities," Duke Zhe said. "Made by perhaps the best potter in history as well — see the ancient rabbit motif? It's the same bowl that the first emperors ate from! A priceless, amazing prize!"

By then, the men had unwrapped the other package. It was an enormous *gang*. The giant porcelain bowl was really a tub, almost as high as Magistrate Tiger's shoulders and twice as wide. Painted on its

surface, graceful blue fish and lotus flowers seemed to weave together in a silent dance.

Magistrate Tiger carefully placed the bowl on the shelf behind him and then stroked the *gang* gently.

"And the *gang*! Made to be an indoor fishpond!" Duke Zhe said. "I was so pleased when you answered the second question and won this. It is perfect for you! Now you will be able to entertain the fish during the winter months as well."

"Also the finest porcelain," Magistrate Tiger said in a gratified voice. "Have you ever seen a *gang* this size, yet so exquisite and thin? They are both truly wondrous gifts."

"But no more than you deserve," Duke Zhe said. "You answered those questions magnificently! Determine the thief by running a race! Share the almond by making it into tea! You answered the emperor's questions so quickly and brilliantly that it was almost as if you knew what the questions were going to be ahead of time."

"Ah," Magistrate Tiger said darkly. "If I had known

the questions ahead of time, I would have been able to answer the emperor's last question."

"My dear friend," Duke Zhe said, "the emperor has asked the question of the snail dispute every year at the Moon Festivities. No one has ever answered it. Neighbors throwing snails in each other's gardens! How could anyone solve that fairly? I think it's an impossible question."

"Perhaps," Magistrate Tiger conceded.

The boy began to sputter. Determine the thief? Sharing an almond? Fighting over snails? His sister quickly pulled him away from the window before he exploded.

"Those were our answers!" he cried as soon as they were out of earshot. "He found out the questions ahead of time and used our answers!"

"Shhh," his sister said, glancing over her shoulder. "It doesn't matter, anyway."

"What do you mean?" the boy said, still outraged. "It was my answer!"

"Well, if everything he does is for you," she said, "then it's okay that he took your answer, right?"

The boy was silent. Did his father roar and trick

and lie for him? He felt a mixture of confusion and resentment.

"It doesn't seem like he does it for me," the boy said sullenly.

"He does," his sister said.

But she sounded more hopeful than sure.

"Another very interesting story, Rendi," Madame Chang said as she nodded slowly.

"Yes!" Peiyi almost shouted. "Too bad the third question was impossible. We could really use the answer. It would solve everything!"

"What do you mean?" Rendi asked.

Master Chao coughed. "Peiyi…" he began.

"It's the whole reason why we hate the Yans and the Yans hate us," Peiyi said, ignoring her father. "Because our ancestors threw snails into each other's gardens."

"The fight between you and Widow Yan is over snails?" Rendi said incredulously.

Master Chao coughed again. "It's not exactly that…" he said.

"Yes, it is!" Peiyi interrupted, her bitterness giving her the courage to speak before her father in a way Rendi had never seen before. "If it wasn't for the snails, then we could be friends with Widow Yan, you and Jiming wouldn't have argued over him marrying MeiLan, and he wouldn't have run away! It's all because no one can answer that silly snail question!"

"I know someone who can answer it," Madame Chang said before Master Chao could erupt with indignation and Rendi could show even more surprise. Everyone stared at her.

"Who?" Rendi asked.

"Mr. Shan," Madame Chang said.

They all turned to Mr. Shan, open-mouthed. Mr. Shan seemed oblivious to the conversation, playing with the toad again. Madame Chang gently touched his shoulder and looked straight into his eyes.

"Mr. Shan," she said, "do you know how to settle the problem of the snails?"

He looked at her, and, again, his eyes seemed to clear like a sky after a storm.

"Of course," Mr. Shan said.

CHAPTER
18

Master Chao, full of skepticism and embarrassment, snorted and left the room before even hearing Mr. Shan's answer. "Good," Mr. Shan said. "If we do it, it's better he doesn't know."

"We are going to do it, right?" Peiyi said, hopping up and down in excitement.

Rendi was surprised to see Madame Chang looking at him. "Are we, Rendi?" she asked him.

Night had come, and already the moans were echoing in Rendi's ears. The sounds were pleading and begging, and Rendi could feel Peiyi's hopeful eyes upon him. Madame Chang's steady gaze refused to release him, and Rendi could not say no. With a silent sigh, he nodded. He would stay until they settled the problem of the snails. What was a few more days?

"Yes," Rendi said. "We'll do it."

Madame Chang smiled, and a look — was it relief? — flashed through her. Did she know? Rendi thought. Did she know he was planning to leave? And why did it matter if he stayed? The sky groaned in answer, and Rendi wrinkled his brow.

However, for the next few days, Rendi had no time to wonder. Although his nights were still full of restless cries, he quickly forgot about them during the day as he, Peiyi, Madame Chang, and Mr. Shan rushed in the hot sun like busy ants.

So when Rendi walked around the wall and to Widow Yan's door, he was full of anticipation. The withered yellow grass crunched like paper offerings under his feet, and Rendi realized that this was the first time he had ever knocked on Widow Yan's door.

Widow Yan, with MeiLan behind her, looked at Rendi

in surprise. The sun cast harsh shadows upon Widow Yan's tired face, and the worried wrinkle between her eyebrows seemed a deep, dark scar. Suddenly, Rendi saw that life had not been easy for Widow Yan and MeiLan, two women living alone in a poor village.

"If he sent you to complain," Widow Yan began, "you tell him —"

"Please," Rendi interrupted, "would you come for tea?"

"Over to the inn?" Widow Yan said. "I wouldn't go to Chao's inn if —"

"No," Rendi interrupted again. "Just to over there." And he beckoned with his arm.

A table straddled the lowest part of the crumbling wall, and the light of the sun directly overhead burned its bare top. A chair rested near the half of the table in Widow Yan's yard, and another chair waited with the other half in Master Chao's yard. The figure of Master Chao, being pulled by Peiyi, was walking toward it.

Widow Yan gave Rendi a questioning look and an amused sniff, but she took his arm as he led her to the table. MeiLan followed, shooting Peiyi curious looks as they came closer. Peiyi, having gotten her father to sit down, grinned at her.

"What is this?" Widow Yan demanded as she let herself be seated. The sharp lines of her face seemed to cut the air as much as her words.

"How should I know?" Master Chao retorted, wiping the dampness from his face, as red as the cinnabar decoration of his belt. "My daughter just dragged me out here. For tea, she says!"

Before Widow Yan could respond, Madame Chang appeared, flanked by Mr. Shan, who was carrying a full tray.

"Welcome," Madame Chang said, as if they were sitting at a banquet table in the emperor's palace instead of their dry, dusty yards in the scorching sun. "Thank you both for honoring us with your presence."

Her gracious words and manner shamed both Widow Yan and Master Chao, and an awkward truce was silently agreed on. Rendi couldn't help smiling to himself as he watched them refrain from making insults to each other for the first time. Madame Chang quickly set down teacups, plates, and chopsticks before them.

She poured the tea, steam misting as the amber liquid filled the rosewood-colored cups. The familiar fragrance wafted in the air and calmed Widow Yan and Master Chao even as they began to flush in the heat. They sipped wordlessly, the black tops of their heads blazing, but the space between them did not seem unfriendly.

However, the silence continued, and Peiyi's second smile at MeiLan was less bright. Peiyi and Rendi slowly brought the small dishes of pork dumplings and fried taro cakes. They looked at each other furtively as Peiyi put down the last dish, which seemed to be filled with small, deep black pearls sprinkled with jade circles of sliced green onions.

"What are these?" Master Chao said, reaching for them with his chopsticks. As he chewed and swallowed, his eyebrows raised, and before he could stop himself, he gasped, "Delicious!"

Curious, Widow Yan took some and found herself closing her eyes in delight. "It is delicious," she said. "It could be served to the emperor himself."

"So you can agree on some things," Madame Chang said. Her words reminded Widow Yan and Master Chao of their dislike for each other, and the stony stillness returned. "If I understand correctly, your first disagreement was over snails?"

The silence snapped.

"If your great-grandfather had not thrown the snails..." Widow Yan spat.

"*My* great-grandfather?!" Master Chao bellowed. "It was *your* ancestor who threw the snails!"

"It was a plague of snails!" Widow Yan said. "He ruined our garden!"

"*Your* snails destroyed our garden," Master Chao said bitterly, "and they are still there. Those disgusting things! No good for anything!"

"Other than causing a quarrel that breaks your families apart?" Madame Chang asked quietly.

Her words were spoken like raindrops, but they fell upon both Master Chao and Widow Yan like an avalanche of stones, forcing them to see thoughts and memories that had been hidden. Insults and words disappeared, and Master Chao found himself thinking of Jiming, whom he had tried hard not to think of since that last slammed door. Master Chao looked down at his teacup, where one drop of liquid sat at the bottom, like a lone tear.

Widow Yan glanced at MeiLan standing beside her. How pale MeiLan was, frail and thin as if the sunlight could be seen through her. When was the last time MeiLan had truly smiled?

The sun shifted over them as if trying to expose a shared secret, and finally Master Chao and Widow Yan looked up. Their eyes met, grief-stricken mirrors of each other's.

"The snails are good for something else too," Mr. Shan said unexpectedly. Master Chao's and Widow Yan's sorrowful thoughts turned to bafflement, for Mr. Shan was looking at them with an amused expression, like a boy watching small dogs play.

"Those snails," he cackled, "those snails are also good to eat!"

Rendi and Peiyi began to laugh as Master Chao and Widow Yan continued to stare. Their laughter had just reached a hysterical pitch when Peiyi gestured to the food they had eaten. "The snails!" she gasped between giggles. "You just ate them!"

"Those are snails?" Master Chao said, slowly

understanding. He took another mouthful, chewing thoughtfully. His face brightened, and his mind began to move with ideas like clicking abacus beads. "If I could serve this..."

"I could add this to my tofu recipe," Widow Yan said. The corners of her mouth began to creep upward as she thought. "I could..."

"You could sell it at the inn," Mr. Shan said with a jovial wave of his arm. They looked at him blankly, and he laughed as if they had told a joke. "The inn sells Widow Yan's food! Then Master Chao gets more customers, and Widow Yan makes more money. Both help each other, and the snails are the best things to grow in the garden after all! Question answered!"

Mr. Shan continued to laugh to himself. He took the toad out of his pocket and began to walk away. Madame Chang smiled and joined him, leaving the others to watch with hopeful eyes.

Master Chao and Widow Yan looked at each other sheepishly. After a moment, Master Chao shrugged, and Widow Yan gave him a small, wry smile. Then Master Chao poured Widow Yan a cup of tea.

CHAPTER
19

Preferring to continue their conversation out of the heat of the sun, Master Chao and Widow Yan walked together into the inn. Their shadows trailed behind them, and when the back door closed, Peiyi and MeiLan began to jump up and down. Even Rendi grinned.

"Now Jiming can come home!" Peiyi squealed. She grabbed MeiLan's waist and danced around her. "You can get married!"

And I can leave, Rendi thought. He looked up at the sun, gleaming in the sky like a burning piece of coal. *It's hot to travel by walking, though. Maybe I'll wait a few more days. It might get cooler.*

"I can't believe it," MeiLan said in dazed delight. "How did this happen?"

"It's because Mr. Shan knew the answer!" Peiyi said. "Rendi told the story and Madame Chang asked Mr. Shan, and now everything is good!"

Rendi could see that MeiLan had no idea what Peiyi was talking about but was too full of happiness to ask for further explanations.

"We have to tell Jiming!" MeiLan said. Suddenly her smile waned, and the brightness in her eyes dimmed. "But how?"

"He'll come back," Peiyi said. "He has to come back, right?"

"I don't know," MeiLan said, and she untangled herself from Peiyi's arms. "We don't even know where he is."

"But..." Peiyi said, and she stopped dancing. MeiLan had already turned and started back to her house.

"Maybe we can find him somehow," MeiLan said, her back toward them. They saw her shoulders sink, and she sounded far from hopeful as she opened the door. "I'll think about it and talk to you later."

"But…" Peiyi said again as MeiLan closed the door behind her. And with a plaintive soft cry, "But Mr. Shan answered the question!"

Peiyi's head drooped, and all signs of her previous joy faded away. Downcast, she began to stack the used dishes on the table. Rendi felt a pang of sadness for her, but her words sparked a sudden curiosity in him.

"Peiyi," Rendi said, emptying the teapot onto the ground, "has Mr. Shan always been this way?"

"What way?" she asked.

"I don't know," he said, struggling to explain. "Kind of crazy. Sometimes he seems half-asleep, but other times he laughs and…answers questions."

"He is more cheerful now," Peiyi said, stopping to consider it. "I never heard him laugh before. He used to always just read a big book and be annoyed at everyone. Jiming used to say he wished Mr. Shan would read a book on manners."

"But he doesn't read anymore," Rendi said. "What happened?"

"I don't know," Peiyi said. "Mr. Shan used to travel too.

Sometimes he'd disappear for months, and then one day he'd show up, reading and not noticing anyone around him again, like he never left. But this last time, Mr. Shan came back without the book."

Rendi frowned. The tea he had poured had already dried up — only a thin line of dampness remained, like a dark thread on the stone ground. What was it that Mr. Shan had said to Madame Chang that first evening? Something about a book . . .

"And I think that's about when he started getting so slow and mixed up," Peiyi said slowly. "It's almost like he's lost sometimes."

"He's like that a lot of the time," Rendi said.

Peiyi squinted at Rendi as if the sun was reflecting off him. "This is the first time you've ever asked me about anybody," she said. "You never seemed to care about anyone else before."

Rendi shrugged, and then, for no reason, he grinned at her. Peiyi's eyes widened, and a small, crooked smile grew on her face in response. Suddenly, they both laughed, and Rendi realized that it was not just Master Chao and Widow Yan who had become friends.

CHAPTER
20

The night continued its moaning, and the day returned to its usual blistering heat. Yes, Rendi thought as he helped Peiyi wash the floors (both of them splashing as much water at each other as they did the ground), it was too hot to leave the village now. If he had to travel by foot, it would be better to wait a week or so.

But right before dinner the next day, when Rendi returned from the Half-Moon Well, a group of fine horses and carriages stood in front of the inn. New guests!

Master Chao, almost twitching with eagerness, met Rendi at the door.

"Take care of the horses," Master Chao said, almost pushing him. "And then hurry back. There are a lot of new guests, and we need your help serving."

Rendi led the horses to the stable, filling all the stalls. He was forced to leave the carriages outside, as there was no room in the small stable, but he was able to inspect them. One carriage, its insides covered with plush cushions and shaded by silk curtains, was obviously to carry the honored guest. The guest must be very wealthy, perhaps even royalty, for the other carriages seemed to be solely for his luggage. There should be plenty of places for Rendi to hide. To leave the Village of Clear Sky, he would not have to walk after all. He could crawl into one of these carriages and ride away, just like he'd originally planned.

Somehow, the thought did not fill Rendi with the happiness he expected. He brushed the horses, frowning. Well, he could help Master Chao and Peiyi with the guests before he left — they needed his help to serve dinner, at the very least. And maybe he could find a way to say goodbye to them. And to Madame Chang and Mr. Shan, and even MeiLan and Widow Yan too. A strange, hard lump seemed to have formed in Rendi's throat, and he had a hard time swallowing.

"Rendi!" a loud whisper called from the back door of the inn. It was Peiyi. "What are you doing? We need your help!"

Rendi put down the horse brush and left the stable. Peiyi stood at the inn's doorway and dragged him inside.

"Hurry," she urged. "Some important government official is here."

Rendi glanced toward the new guests. The government official clearly was very important; companions who could only be his servants and guards flanked him on all sides. The only things Rendi could see of the important government official were his silk robes and his pale, thin hands, which looked as if they had never held anything heavier than a lute.

Impressed by the guest's obvious high stature, Master Chao was filled with nervousness. He had filled a jug with wine, and the liquid made tiny waves as his hands trembled. It was Son Wine, the wine Master Chao had bought from the merchant so long ago, Rendi thought with a pang, but he said nothing. Master Chao jumped and almost spilled the wine when two new guests, dusty-looking traders, entered.

"More guests?" Peiyi said to Rendi. She sighed as the travelers insisted on the first-floor room in the center of the inn. "And superstitious ones too."

"What do you mean?" Rendi asked.

"Ghosts are supposed to gather in the rooms at the ends of the inn." Peiyi snorted. "Superstitious guests always want rooms in the middle."

Rendi grinned, but their conversation was cut short as Master Chao rushed toward them. "Rendi," Master Chao said, pushing the jug of wine toward him, "serve this."

"Shouldn't I look after their animals?" Rendi asked, motioning at the traders.

Master Chao looked around at the busy dining room. Madame Chang and Mr. Shan had also seated themselves at a table. He grimaced. "Serve the wine," he said, "then take care of their animals. And hurry!"

Rendi spun around quickly, running into one of the superstitious traders walking to another table. The trader's belt had a tiger's paw hanging from it, and it swung toward Rendi as if trying to claw him. He stumbled to the official's table, barely keeping the wine from tipping.

"Careful, boy," one of the men said with a grin. "We'll have to behead you if you spill on us."

"Beheading?" another man bantered. "I'd think drawing and quartering would be more appropriate."

"That's true," the man agreed with mocking thoughtfulness. "There should be torture and death for insulting the men of Duke Zhe!"

Rendi's head jerked up, and with horror, he stared at the government official, Magistrate Tiger's friend, Duke Zhe.

CHAPTER
21

Rendi quickly glanced around him. Peiyi and Master Chao were busy working in the kitchen, and Madame Chang and Mr. Shan seemed to be in their own conversation. Rendi took a deep breath and turned back to the table, where Duke Zhe met his still-panicked eyes with a benevolent smile.

"Come, now. Look, you've scared the poor boy," Duke Zhe said to his companions. "You know these peasant folk will believe anything. Look at that village we passed yesterday with the dog bride."

The men laughed, and Rendi could do nothing except continue to gape, confusion flickering over his face.

"You've never heard of it?" the duke said, mistaking Rendi's expression. "Perhaps it is just a local custom. The villagers dress up a dog as a bride, in a red gown and the finest jewelry they can afford, and then stage a wedding."

"They even put the dog in the covered sedan chair," hooted one of the men, "and had the long procession — it was a big parade with the entire village! Just like a real wedding!"

"It's all for those in the Starry River above," Duke Zhe said. "They hope that it makes them laugh so hard that they cry and then rain will fall."

"These peasants are trying all sorts of things to make it rain," another man said. "The whole way here, I've been seeing all kinds of superstitious appeals. Putting stone carvings in the hot sun to make them suffer, burning smoke in front of statues hoping their eyes will water, throwing dirt on dragon figures..."

"What's that one for?" Duke Zhe asked with an amusement that made one of the traders scowl.

"To make the dragon bring rain so he can clean himself," the man hooted. "But there's a drought happening everywhere but here. This is the first clean cup I've seen in a while."

"It has been very dry here," Master Chao said, who had by this time come out of the kitchen with Peiyi. "But our village wells still have water."

"There must be something unusual about this place, then," one of the traders said with eyes that looked at them with something like suspicion. He fingered the talisman on his belt. Instead of a tiger's paw like his companion's, his was a circle made from a coffin nail. "Everywhere else is running out of water and begging for rain."

"Rendi," Peiyi whispered to him. She had come over with chopsticks and plates to put on the duke's table. "Do you remember when you filled in the well and my father said he thought everyone else's well would go dry soon? They didn't go dry. Why?"

Rendi tried to shrug.

"It stayed hot, and it didn't rain. Do you think there is something here that keeps the water from disappearing?"

Peiyi said. "Nothing changed, except Madame Chang coming. But that wouldn't do anything, would it?"

Rendi could not even shake his head, and finally Peiyi gave him a puzzled look, now more confused about his uninterest than her questions. But Rendi felt frozen, barely able to move, much less talk. All he could do was continue to pour the wine, his knuckles turning white around the jug.

CHAPTER
22

"The other villages sound quite desperate," Madame Chang said from the next table. Somehow her quiet voice could be heard clearly, even despite the guffaws of the duke's men. "It sounds as if they need help."

"Uh...er, yes," the duke said uncomfortably. "Too bad I am too busy trying to help find missing people instead."

"Missing people?" Master Chao had come over to push Rendi toward the table of the two traders and stopped as he heard the duke's words. "My son is missing."

"I'm searching for a magistrate's son," the duke said with a faint tone of admonishment.

Rendi gulped and clutched the cup he was passing to one of the traders, the one with the tiger's paw. The man looked at him carefully as he firmly took the cup away.

"Of course, of course," Master Chao said, bowing with embarrassment.

"Two sons, one moon," Mr. Shan said. "All missing."

"How old are these missing boys?" the trader called out, ignoring Mr. Shan's words about the moon.

"Oh, my son is not a boy," Master Chao said, bowing again, but this time with a hint of wistful sadness. "Jiming is a grown man — or at least he thinks he is."

"The magistrate's son is a boy, however," the duke said with dignity. "A young boy who has probably been kidnapped."

"Kidnapped?" Rendi gasped before he could stop himself.

"Yes," Duke Zhe said gravely. "His father is quite upset. I'm conducting this search as a favor for him. It seems it needed the attention of his superiors. The magistrate has already decreed that anyone found with the boy will be arrested and punished, but his men have found nothing. Poor fellow. His worry has made him into quite a different person — one day I came over unannounced to find him shouting and roaring like a tiger. I even overheard someone calling him Magistrate Tiger."

"Magistrate Tiger?" Peiyi asked. Her eyes widened, and Rendi felt as if an iron shirt were being tightened around him as Peiyi continued. "But...he's in the story..."

"Story?" Duke Zhe asked.

"There is a story about a tiger that this magistrate should probably hear," Madame Chang said before Peiyi could say anything else. She looked at Rendi out of the corner of her eye. "Would you like to hear it?"

"Why not?" Duke Zhe said. "We must let the horses rest for the evening anyway."

THE STORY OF THE WHITE TIGER

L ong ago, when mountains wandered regularly and before the six suns appeared in the sky, a tiger terrorized a village. This tiger was no ordinary tiger. Not only was it the largest tiger ever seen by the villagers, it was a peculiar color. It was white, a dirty, pasty white, the color of clothes worn at a funeral. This was appropriate, for the tiger brought death with it. Whatever the tiger did not kill right away died soon after from being cut with its claws. Even the famous five poisons of the snake, scorpion, toad, centipede, and spider combined were not as deadly as the poisonous claws of the White Tiger. It fed on the village's sheep and cattle at whim, and everyone knew that one of the villagers themselves would soon be the tiger's victim. "We must destroy the White Tiger!" they said to one another. "But how?"

As they did for many things, they consulted the old sage who lived on a mountaintop nearby. But when they described the fierce White Tiger and asked how they could destroy it, the old sage only stroked his beard and consulted the large book in his lap. Finally, the sage said, "I will have to see the tiger myself. Take me to it."

The villagers looked at one another, and slowly they led the sage down the mountain, past a tall tree and lake, and to a dark hole, like a cave, in one of the hills around their village. By this time, night had fallen, and the hole looked as black and as evil as the mouth of a dangerous beast.

"The White Tiger lives in there," the villagers whispered. "We dare not go any farther."

"Well, I must go in and see it," the old man said. "Will no one accompany me?"

The villagers looked at one another until finally a young man, the village's potter, stepped forward. The old sage nodded at him, pleased. Together, they walked into the dark hole, the light of a lantern shaking in the potter's hand. At the end, the White Tiger lay asleep, looking even larger and more ferocious in the dim light. The old man gazed at the tiger thoughtfully.

"It is as I thought," he said. "See how the stripes on his forehead make the symbol for the word *wang*? A symbol of power? It is impossible for you to destroy this tiger."

"Then we are doomed!" the young potter cried.

The sage held his fingers to his lips to quiet the man and led him out of the cave to their village. The villagers gathered around them, only to wail in despair as the sage repeated his words.

"But the tiger must be killed!" the villagers said. "How can we save our village?"

"I can help you do that," the sage said. "But I will need a baby."

"A baby?" the villager said. "For what?"

"For the tiger," the sage said. "It will not be harmed."

His words brought the village to an uproar. A baby for the tiger! The sage was crazy! No one would give up a child to the tiger. No matter what the sage said, the baby would just be an easy meal for such a wicked beast. Finally, the potter spoke up.

"We will not sacrifice a baby to the tiger," the young man said. At home, he had a baby daughter and he would never dream of giving her to the tiger. "We would rather die first."

The old sage nodded. "I expected as much," he said. "I will try a substitute. It should be enough to save your village, but it will not completely cure the White Tiger. Bring me a bowl."

This the young man quickly did, giving the sage one of his handmade bowls. The old sage walked to the lake, a sheet of rippling silk, with the young man and the other villagers following. At the lake's edge, the sage picked a tall blade of grass with a drop of dew hanging from it like a tiny crystal berry. In the moonlight, the water droplet turned a sparkling silver, and the old man cast it into the lake.

The villagers could not help crowding around the old sage as he bent over the lake water. As the dewdrop fell into the water, it darkened to a black silhouette and began to swim. The dew had turned into a tadpole!

But before the villagers could even gasp in awe, the old man scooped up the tadpole with the bowl. He flipped it over on top of the ground, water spreading from the bowl's edges like fingers on an opening hand. Then the sage looked up at the moon and knocked his walking stick against the bowl.

The thick, dark bowl cracked into pieces as if it were an eggshell, and under the broken pieces, something wriggled. The old man lifted off the shards of pottery, revealing a baby rabbit as pale as the moon above.

The sage took the baby rabbit in his hands, and a smaller, more helpless creature could not have existed. He smiled at it, and the baby rabbit opened its black eyes, which gleamed like the night water of the lake. The old man and the rabbit stared at each other as if a silent understanding had been shared, and then the sage walked back to the cave of the White Tiger, the villagers watching silently.

At the mouth of the cave, the sage gently laid down the baby rabbit and walked away.

When he reached the waiting villagers, they began to press the sage with questions and worries. "Why did you leave the rabbit there?" they asked. "The White Tiger will just kill it!"

The sage said nothing. He slowly gestured. Dawn

was breaking, and a grumble echoed from the dark hole. The villagers went silent. The White Tiger had awakened!

The White Tiger came out of its hole and immediately saw the baby rabbit, a helpless mound of soft fur trembling in the morning light. The tiger snarled, its dangerous, evil claws extended, and the villagers gasped in horror. But suddenly, the tiger's paw froze in mid-air, and the rabbit and the tiger stared at each other. The baby rabbit made no sound, but the tiger put its paw on the ground. Gently, the tiger sniffed it and, like a cat, licked the rabbit's face. Then the tiger scooped up the rabbit with its paw and carried it back into the cave.

The villagers stared in disbelief. The old man turned toward his mountain and began to walk away.

"Where are you going?" the villagers asked. "What about the tiger?"

"Leave a gourd of milk in front of the cave every day for six weeks," the old man said without turning around, "and your village will be saved."

"But you didn't kill the White Tiger!" they said.

"I never said I was going to kill it," the old man said, and continued walking.

The villagers did as the old man said. Every morning, they left a gourd of milk by the cave, and strangely, the tiger did stop bothering them. On the last day of the six weeks, out of curiosity, the young potter climbed the tall tree after leaving the milk. In a few moments, the tiger ambled out of the cave. Was it the same tiger? It was still white, but now, instead of the grayish-white of a choking smoke, the tiger was a clean, pure white like the light of the moon. The baby rabbit was the same color and looked healthy and fat as it hopped out. It eagerly drank the milk as the tiger tipped the gourd with its...hands? The man thought he saw fingers instead of claws on the tiger's paws. He blinked his eyes. Impossible!

The rabbit and the tiger disappeared back into the cave, and when the man returned to the village to tell of what he had seen, no one believed him. "Leave the White Tiger alone," they told him. "With any luck, it will just disappear."

And it seemed that the villagers' wish was answered.

The potter was the last to ever see the tiger and the baby rabbit. Villagers began to forget about the White Tiger, only mentioning it as a whispered story.

But about nine years later, a group of village children, including the potter's daughter, ran to their parents shouting with excitement.

"We were playing in the tall grass by the lake," the oldest boy told his mother, "when a huge snake slithered from the grass, hissing!"

"It was going to attack me," the potter's daughter said to her father, her eyes round. "Everyone screamed and screamed."

"And, then, out of nowhere, something rushed out, grabbed the snake, and threw it away!" the boy continued, his words becoming shouts. "The thing that threw the snake...I think it was a monster!"

"Yes," another girl said, almost sobbing. "It had human legs and arms, but its head and chest looked like...like...a *tiger*!"

"It even had a tiger tail!" another boy said.

The parents did their best to calm the children, but

they looked at one another with worry and bewilderment. A monster? Half-man, half-tiger? What kind of strange beast had come? They would have to hunt it down and destroy it.

But the potter, now a bearded, middle-aged man, wondered. "Before we try to kill it," he said to the villagers, "let us ask the old sage who lives on the mountain."

The villagers agreed, and they again traveled to see the old sage. When they asked him if they should kill the beast, the old sage looked quite annoyed.

"You want to kill the White Tiger again?" he said, disgusted. "I told you this was the only way to save your village."

"But if this beast is the White Tiger," the bearded man said, "how can we save our village from it?"

"Fools! All of you!" the sage said. "You do not need to save your village from the White Tiger! The White Tiger will save your village."

"But...how..." the villagers began. However, the sage had turned away, muttering to himself, "I believe I will have to start limiting these questions. I think next century I will start answering only once a decade, or maybe once every ninety-nine years..."

The villagers returned home, and for the next nine years, sightings of the strange beast continued. One time, it saved a raft full of children from drowning in the lake. Then it cleared boulders that had fallen in a landslide. And it carried a lost calf back to the herd. Each time the beast was seen, the description of it changed. It didn't have a tiger's tail. Its chest was human hair, not fur. Only its head was like a tiger.

And one day, the potter, his beard now gray, returned from a journey with a new kind of clay he was very excited about. He was not sure, but he suspected it would be able to make pots and bowls that could be pure white and painted as never before. He was in such a rush to return that he almost did not see his daughter as he hurried into the wilderness that lay before the entrance of the village. She seemed to be alone, except for a rabbit in her arms.

"What are you doing here?" he asked her.

"Waiting for you," she said, but her pale moon-colored face flushed. She set down the rabbit and walked her father back to the village. The potter looked at her. She had always been different from the other village children — always quiet, as if she were constantly listening to whispers in the wind. His head filled with questions, but he said nothing.

However, he did not have to wonder long. One day, while he was working on a new bowl design, his daughter walked into the village with one hand holding the jade-white rabbit and the other holding the arm of a strange young man.

The young man was, by far, the strongest and handsomest man the villagers had ever seen. There was something striking about him. He had a powerful, magnetic air, and all stared and gathered around him. He would like to make his home in the village, the young man said, promising to be a hard worker, a help to all who needed it. Also, while he had nothing more to give but his pet rabbit, the man said as he bowed humbly before the gray-bearded man, he would be honored to marry the potter's daughter.

At that, all the village maidens looked at the potter's daughter with jealousy while the rest of the villagers burst into cheers of welcome. All rejoiced at having such a noble, valiant young man in their community, except for the gray-bearded potter. He had noticed what the other villagers had not.

"That is an interesting scar you have," the potter said, motioning to the faint mark on the young man's forehead. "It looks like the symbol of power."

"Yes," the man said. "I've always had it."

The graybeard said nothing for a long moment, and his daughter's hopeful eyes dimmed. But then he began to paint a rabbit on the bowl he was working on, and her smile shined with joy. He looked at her and nodded, welcoming the man into his family and the village.

"The mark of power! He was WangYi!" Peiyi whispered. "He saved the village by shooting down the suns... That's why he was so powerful..."

"It was a very interesting story," Duke Zhe said over Peiyi's murmurs. "But I don't see why you thought it was something my magistrate friend should hear."

"I thought that was obvious," Madame Chang said. "If kindness and compassion can turn a tiger into a man, then the opposite must be true."

"In the blood," Mr. Shan said, and Rendi was surprised to see that Mr. Shan was nodding at him. "The blood that pumps in you can be of man or tiger. The heart decides."

"I guess this son of the magistrate should watch out, then," one of the traders called out boisterously. "His dad could turn into a tiger!"

The room filled with titters and laughter, but Rendi felt as if he couldn't breathe. He caught the trader looking at him slyly and was glad to escape to the horses.

CHAPTER

23

Since the duke's horses took up all the room in the stable, Rendi was forced to leave the traders' animals tethered to a picket outside. The traders also had horses, which was unusual, as most merchants had donkeys with carts or heavy-laden camels. But Rendi did not have much time to think about it. Collecting enough water for all the horses and the new guests kept Rendi so busy that he didn't even have time to get his own dinner. But he didn't mind. He wasn't hungry. And he preferred not to return to the dining room.

Still, the tightness inside him did not loosen much. Duke Zhe's appearance had been a shock. Now, instead of wishing to stow away in one of the carriages, Rendi hoped the duke would just leave quickly, without him. He closed his eyes and sighed, and he left the stable, feeling confused.

He was not the only one confused. As he shut the stable door behind him, Rendi saw an outline of a shuffling figure against the setting sun, the croaking sound of a toad making accompanying music. Mr. Shan was beginning to walk across the bare stone plain.

"Mr. Shan!" Rendi said, running to him. "What are you doing?"

"I'm trying to remember," Mr. Shan said. He pressed his fingers against his bearded chin. "Without the moon, I've forgotten everything. I even forgot that I forgot."

"Mr. Shan?" Rendi said, concerned. What was he saying? Was he crazy?

"I had forgotten I had lost it until she reminded me," Mr. Shan said, staring into the distance with eyes that did not see Rendi. "I have to find it."

Rendi followed Mr. Shan's gaze into the miles of the

stone field, an empty stretch of shadows. The toad, its eyes bulging above Mr. Shan's pocket, stared. The sky made a mournful noise, the first lonely echo of the night.

"You shouldn't go out there now," Rendi said, taking Mr. Shan's arm. "Let me take you home."

"Home," Mr. Shan said absently. "I have not had a home for a long time."

Yet he allowed Rendi to turn him around and lead him back to the winding street. Mr. Shan offered no more strange words, and except for the toad's occasional song and the hollow thumping of Mr. Shan's walking stick, all was quiet. But Rendi was filled with questions. He couldn't believe that Mr. Shan — who knew the answer to the problem of the snails, whom Madame Chang held in high regard — was crazy. But his words didn't make any sense either. Wasn't the house Mr. Shan lived in his home? Was it Madame Chang who reminded him what he had forgotten? What was it he was looking for? And what did it have to do with the moon?

Mr. Shan's small house near the Inn of Clear Sky seemed no different from any of the other villagers', which was perhaps why Rendi had only glanced at it before. The rows of scalloped tiles that made up the roof looked more like tree ear mushrooms than stone. Grass and weeds, yellowed from lack of water, grew between the rough-hewed rocks of the walls. The shadows that fell from the dimming light seemed to make the house disappear into the sky, but there was nothing unusual about it.

"Mr. Shan," Rendi finally said, as they reached the front of the house, "what did you mean about the moon?"

"The moon?" Mr. Shan said in his vague way. "The moon means peace. It is the image of harmony and peace."

Rendi tried again. "You said without the moon, you forgot everything. And you said that you didn't have a home."

"Yes," Mr. Shan said. "You cannot have a home without peace."

The night groaned, and Rendi gave up. Mr. Shan lit a small lantern outside his door. As Mr. Shan stepped over the raised doorway, he looked at Rendi, the flame in his lantern looking like a small, blooming flower.

"You want to go home, Rendi," Mr. Shan said. "You should go."

Rendi turned and walked back to the inn, full of more

questions and confused thoughts. When Mr. Shan had bidden him off, Rendi had looked beyond him into his house, visible by the lit lantern. The house had been completely empty. There was not a table or stool or bed. The only thing Rendi had seen in that bare room was a blue cloth bag that lay forlorn in the corner. Perhaps that was where Mr. Shan kept his money? *He eats every day at the inn*, Rendi thought, *and he always pays. Is that all he has?*

Rendi sighed as he reached the front of the inn. Thinking of Mr. Shan had taken his mind off the new guests. The bright windows and the lit lanterns of the inn looked like a necklace of jewels, and Rendi felt the tightness in his throat returning. He looked behind him at the last sliver of light on the horizon, and the sky gave a painful wail that echoed in his ears.

Then a rough arm grabbed him! Rendi jolted backward, and his feet were thrown in the air. Before he could think to yell, a large hand clamped over his mouth.

A voice snarled in his ear, "Got you!"

CHAPTER

24

"I tell you, Fang, he's the missing boy!" the man said.

"He doesn't look like any rich man's son," the other man, obviously Fang, said, scowling.

Rendi stared at them. In the dim light, they seemed more like figures in a nightmare. Nothing seemed real. But he was truly there, inside one of the rooms of the inn with his hands and feet tied. After the trader had dropped him on the floor like a sack of rice, Rendi had propped himself against the wall, drooling into the coarse cloth knotted over his mouth. The gag was unnecessary, for Rendi was so shocked, he could not make a sound.

"Besides, Liu, he isn't part of the plan," Fang said. He was older than the other, the bristles of his unshaven face were gray like the ashes of burned offerings, and his words fell with the weight of weariness. But even more than his words, the cold, ruthless look in his eyes belied his being a trader. "We want the duke's strings of gold, not some stray kid."

"This kid's worth more than the duke's traveling cash," Liu said. "Think how much we'll get ransoming him to that magistrate."

Fang scanned Rendi as if he were a calf for sale. With an unsympathetic tug, he jerked Rendi forward.

"Look at his hands," Fang said, shining the lantern over Rendi's hands, calloused and scarred from his frequent work at the well. "Those aren't the hands of a rich boy."

"I tell you, it's him! I saw his face when the duke was talking," Liu insisted. "And if he's not, he knows something about it!"

Liu pushed Rendi back against the wall, thrust a lantern in front of his face, and sneered, "Right, boy?"

Rendi stared back as the two men peered into his face, strangely grateful that he couldn't answer with the gag in his mouth. But even without speaking, he couldn't hide his look of guilt and fear.

"Fine," Fang said grudgingly. "We'll get the duke's money tonight as planned and take the boy with us. If he isn't the magistrate's son, we'll get what he knows and get rid of him."

Rendi shivered and tried not to think about how they would "get rid of him" if they chose to. Liu nodded, and Fang looked out the window into the night. Moments passed, and Rendi could barely hear the moans of the night over the thumping of his blood in his ears.

"Village of Clear Sky! Bah!" Fang said, spitting on the ground. "This place should be called the Village of Black Sky! There's nothing out there but black. Even the stars aren't out tonight."

"Did you see that thing they call the Stone Pancake?" Liu said, joining Fang at the window. "Nothing but flat, dead rock for miles."

"I don't like this place. There's something about it. That lady talking about tigers changing into men has me spooked," Fang said. He spat on the ground again. "I have a feeling this inn is cursed."

The sky made another cry, and Rendi wondered if it was the wailing that was affecting Fang and Liu. But the men gazed into the blank blackness, obviously not hearing a sound. As the night groaned, Rendi tried to work the bonds around his wrists. But the rope was as tight as the clamped claws of a crab.

"We're out tonight, anyway," Fang said. "You took care of the guards?"

"I put enough stuff in their wine that any of the duke's men will be lucky if they wake up by tomorrow afternoon," Liu said. "You didn't drink any, did you?"

"What am I, a fool?" Fang said.

A soft knock sounded at the door.

"Quick!" said Fang, cocking his head. "Hide the kid!"

Rendi was thrust in the corner of the room behind the door. Liu piled their coats on top of him. "One sound out of you," he hissed, "and you'll be sorry, rich boy."

Rendi gulped. As the door opened, he could see only the worn and dirty embroidered goldfish of Peiyi's slippers.

"My father wanted to know if you needed more oil for your lanterns," Peiyi said. "He can bring it up with your night wine and snack."

"We didn't order any night wine," Fang said.

"It's complimentary," Peiyi said, as if she was reciting, "to thank our guests for visiting the Inn of Clear Sky. We hope you come again."

"Oh," Liu said, clearly amused. "All right, then. But make sure it's a fresh jar of wine. We don't want that same stuff that was served at dinner, do we, Fang?"

Fang didn't answer. He seemed much more interested in something else. He stepped forward.

"What's that on your forehead?" Fang asked Peiyi. "Why do you have the *wang* symbol written there?"

"It's protection," Peiyi said.

"I know," Fang said, "but it's not the Day of Five Poisons. Why do you need protection now?"

"I'm not supposed to talk about it to guests..." Peiyi started, her voice quavering.

"Tell me, girl!" Fang growled impatiently.

"One of the five poisons is here all the time!" Peiyi said in a scared whisper. "The Noxious Toad... it haunts this place!"

"The Noxious Toad?" Fang said. "The toad with blood eyes? With the poison vapor?"

"Yes," Peiyi said, her voice almost impossible to hear. "If you breathe its poison, you die."

Underneath the coats, Rendi wrinkled his brow. What was Peiyi talking about? The Noxious Toad of the Day of Five Poisons? The only toad that plagued them was the one Mr. Shan played with. Was she trying to give him a message? But how could she? Peiyi didn't even know these traders were thieves and kidnappers, much less that Rendi was tied up behind the door. Should he try to warn her? Maybe she could get help? The night made a sad whimper, and Rendi was silent. Small Peiyi was no match for these men. Anything he did would put her in danger too.

"The wine!" Liu said. "You're not giving us that wine for hospitality, are you? You mixed realgar in the wine, didn't you? To make sure we won't be poisoned?"

"It's... it's... it's complimentary," Peiyi stuttered. Rendi could feel their glares, and he could see that even Peiyi's feet were shaking.

"Tell your father we want that wine quick," Fang said finally in a voice so cutting Rendi could imagine it drawing blood. "A fresh jar, remember. Now!"

The shabby goldfish slippers scurried away, and the door shut with an angry thud.

"Noxious Toad!" Fang spat. "I knew this place was cursed!"

CHAPTER
25

For the next few minutes, Rendi heard only a torrent of curses and swears. The coats on top of him smelled of stale wine, and he felt like a sweltering chicken in a pot. Rendi was almost glad when Liu kicked the coats off him and propped him up.

"Did you know about this poison toad, boy?" he demanded. Rendi's arms were sticky with sweat, and Liu, repulsed, quickly dropped him to the ground. The gag, loosened from the perspiration that coated his face, drooped off, and Rendi was unsure whether he should answer.

"Is it true about the toad?" Fang growled.

"No…" Rendi started.

"Don't lie to us," Liu said with a glower.

"I mean, no one knows," Rendi said, his mind racing for a lie. What had Peiyi gotten him into? The lantern light wavered, and Rendi looked at Fang's and Liu's faces above him. The sky screeched, and a wave of reckless anger swept over him. Scum, both of them! Why not scare them? "No one knows where or when the toad will come with its poison. It's like a ghost toad."

"Ghost toad," Liu repeated.

"Yes," Rendi said, starting to enjoy himself. Telling stories for Madame Chang had given him good practice. "It's worse than the Noxious Toad of the Day of Five Poisons. Maybe it's the ghost of the first Noxious Toad, because it appears out of nowhere at any time with red eyes dripping blood."

The night sighed, and the light of the lanterns flickered violently. Fang and Liu looked at each other. Rendi continued.

"This toad's noxious vapor is worse too," Rendi said, lowering his voice to a hushed whisper. "When it opens its mouth, the room fills with a disgusting, foul smell, and it poisons you until you die a horrible death. You choke, and your skin tightens and turns wrinkled and covered with warts, and your eyes bulge until you're blind, and then you die!"

Suddenly, the flames of the lanterns disappeared, one immediately after the other, leaving the room in blackness. Liu and Fang gasped in horror while Rendi, invisible in the dark, smiled with satisfaction. He had been watching the wavering, dying light and had timed his words just right.

Fang lit a match. Even in the dim light, Rendi could see his face was white as he reached for the lantern and cursed.

"It's out of oil," he spat in angry annoyance.

"Maybe it's the Noxious Toad ghost," Rendi said, trying to keep the amusement out of his voice.

"Gag that boy up again!" Fang said, glaring. He rummaged in his small bag and then lit a candle. "I don't like this," he grumbled to himself.

Liu replaced Rendi's gag, but his eyes watched Fang.

"You think we should forget the duke?" Liu asked.

"The horses are already waiting. Maybe we just take the kid and get out of here now. We'll still make money. I swear we'll get it off the boy."

Fang looked at Rendi, the candle flame casting long and distorted shadows over him. The wind whimpered in the darkness.

"He isn't a sure thing," Fang said, slowly shaking his head. "In an hour, the duke and his men will be sleeping like stones, if they aren't already. We'll get the gold and leave."

"You sure?" Liu said.

Fang nodded, his hand rubbing the coffin-nail ring again. "In the meantime, we'll get that wine. The innkeeper thinks it's enough protection."

"He better be right," Liu said.

Rendi's feelings of gratification were quickly draining away. No matter what happened, Fang and Liu were going to take him. He needed to think of a way out. Would Fang and Liu leave him in the room while they went after the duke's money? Maybe Rendi could get Peiyi and Master Chao to hear him...Master Chao! He was coming with the wine! Rendi could alert him! Though it wasn't really fair. Rendi thought about short, soft Master Chao, whose belly was like a stuffed dumpling. Master Chao was only a better match for Fang and Liu when compared with Peiyi. But Rendi was starting to feel desperate.

As if on cue, there was a knock at the door.

"It must be the innkeeper with the wine," Liu said. Both men stood up and went to the door, Rendi forgotten. As Fang opened the door, the dim light from the hallway cascaded in like a gliding ghost. Rendi heard Master Chao's voice, polite and proper. "Good evening. Your complimentary night wine?"

"It's not complimentary," Fang growled as he took a step forward, the door blocking him from Rendi's view. "We know what it's for!"

This is my only chance! Rendi thought. The black sky screamed in agreement, and Rendi began to kick at the wall with his bound feet, as hard as he could. "Master Chao!" he tried to yell through the gag. "Help!"

Liu strode over to Rendi and, with a swift sweep of his arms, grabbed him — easily forcing him to be still.

"Is something wrong?" Master Chao asked.

"Master Chao!" Rendi tried to yell again, the gag making his words just a mumble of noises. Liu took a coat and threw it over Rendi's head.

"Nothing's wrong, except for your cursed inn!" Fang said loudly. He pretended to look behind him. "Our lanterns don't even have oil, and we have to trip around in the dark. What kind of inn is this?"

"I'm sorry, I'm sorry," Master Chao said humbly. "I thought you had enough lantern oil. I will go get some immediately."

"Forget it," Fang said. "The less we see your face, the better we'll feel. Just give me the wine, and leave us alone."

Rendi could hear the clinking of glasses on a tray as Fang took it, and a sick, nauseated feeling overcame him. Master Chao was leaving! The night howled in his ears, and Rendi gave one last struggle, pushing the coat off his head, but Liu's strong arms fixed him firmly. Rendi could do nothing but watch the faint light draw away as the door closed with a solid bang, like the lid of a coffin.

CHAPTER

26

As soon as the door closed, Liu grabbed Rendi off the ground and shook him violently. "That was really stupid, rich boy," Liu sneered. "Really stupid!" He threw Rendi on the ground and was about to strike him when Fang grabbed his arm.

"Later," Fang said. "The last thing we need is some blubbering kid making more noise. That peacock of an innkeeper was curious enough."

Fang had put the tray on the small table near the door, but it could barely be seen in the blackness of the room.

The sounds of the night had lessened to a miserable whine, and the wavering candlelight did little more than cast shadows, leaving the room as dark as the inside of a tomb.

"Fine." Liu nodded, giving Rendi a menacing glare, which looked even more malevolent in the flickering light. He gave Rendi's legs a silent, but not gentle, kick and followed Fang back across the room.

Fang brought the candle closer to the table, and Rendi could see that the tray was full. Master Chao had been unusually generous, for not only was there a jug of wine and two cups, but an assortment of covered dishes, the largest big enough to hold a roasted chicken. Rendi frowned in puzzlement. Had Master Chao ever given a complimentary meal like this before?

"That pudgy innkeeper will have enough to think about after we leave," Liu said with a sneering laugh. "Did I tell you about that last one, the prince we robbed the same way? They arrested all the inn workers — from the cook to the owner. Ha!"

"Since we're taking the boy, this time they'll think he did it," Fang said, but he obviously wasn't that interested.

He looked out the window again. "You can't see a thing out there. The horses are ready, right?"

"Everything's right outside the door," Liu said. "Horses, packs...just waiting for us to grab the gold and go."

Was what Fang said true? In the morning, when the duke saw that the gold was missing, they would see that Rendi had disappeared too. Maybe the duke would realize he had been drugged, and Peiyi and Master Chao and Madame Chang would remember that Rendi had poured the wine! They would think he was the thief, and they would all hate him, he thought. And he wouldn't be able to explain or tell them the truth. He would be gone! All this time, Rendi had been trying to leave the Village of Clear Sky, and now all he wished was to stay. Suddenly, the emptiness in his stomach seemed to become a hole swallowing him, and the sky's sadness, his own. A single tear, like a sliver of stone, leaked from his eye.

"We better drink that wine," Fang said, turning back from the window. Rendi watched as Liu sat down, looking at the full tray with greedy eyes.

"And eat," Liu said, lifting the cover off the largest platter. "Let's see what the..."

Liu's voice died away as a disgusting, vile odor filled the air. His arm froze, holding the platter cover, and all eyes bulged as they saw what lay underneath.

It was a large, glowing toad. Eerie greenish lights quivered inside its grotesque belly, like trapped spirits. It sat in a pool of evil reddish-black liquid, with bubbling warts and dark-stained lines dripping from its eyes. Those swollen eyes stared, and the foul, revolting odor made Rendi's eyes water.

"The Noxious Toad!" Fang whispered.

The toad opened its mouth. A tiny light shot out of it only to be snatched back by the toad's gruesome tongue. "*EERRR-rripp!*" the toad bellowed.

Fang and Liu screamed. The table and the tray were kicked over, and all Rendi could hear was the mad panic of clattering dishes and curses as the men climbed over each other to reach the door. They shouted and swore and sobbed in terror. Finally, the door jerked open, and fresh air and faint light beckoned. There was no hesitation. With the night shrieking, Fang and Liu raced out of the room, out of the inn, and into the black night, riding their hidden horses as fast as they could so that they could leave the Inn of Clear Sky far, far behind them.

CHAPTER
27

Rendi stared. A pale rectangle of light streamed from the hallway onto the wreckage of broken dishware and splattered wine. But the room was empty. Fang and Liu had left. Without him. Rendi was filled with shocked disbelief.

Then, like an exploding firecracker, the room burst with light and lanterns and people and sound.

"Rendi! Rendi! Are you all right?" Peiyi said. Noises and words mixed together, and the bright lights blinded him. When he was finally able to see, a crowd of faces was looking down at him. They were the faces of Peiyi,

Master Chao, Madame Chang, Mr. Shan, and even Widow Yan and MeiLan. He blinked at them, feeling as if he had just awakened from a nightmare.

"I'll get that," Master Chao said, cutting the bonds on Rendi's arms. Widow Yan untied his feet, and Madame Chang removed the gag. Peiyi kept talking, her jumbled words like a rushing river.

"We saw them grab you — me and Madame Chang saw it from her window," Peiyi said. "And I didn't know what to do, but Madame Chang told me to get Mr. Shan, and then he told us to get Widow Yan's fermented tofu and have the toad swallow some fireflies and paint the *wang* symbol on my forehead, and we could fake the Noxious Toad..."

"What?" Rendi said in bewilderment, his mind still dazed. They had faked the Noxious Toad? The revolting smell of the noxious vapor was Widow Yan's tofu? The eerie, glowing toad was Mr. Shan's toad with a firefly dinner? Rendi was too bewildered to laugh.

"We knew the men were superstitious, so Mr. Shan said scaring them away would be the best way to save you," Peiyi continued. "I was so scared! Why did they take you, Rendi? What did they want you for? My father melted his cinnabar belt decoration to make the blood — did I tell you that part?"

"What?" Rendi said again. Peiyi was asking questions faster than he could answer, but Rendi was glad. He wasn't sure he knew how to answer them.

"Peiyi," MeiLan said, "you can tell Rendi the details later."

"Yes," Master Chao said, helping Rendi stagger onto his feet. Rendi's legs felt stiff and sore, as if he hadn't moved in days. "Let's go downstairs."

As Rendi stood in a room full of golden light and people, a room that had just moments before been nothing but darkness, he suddenly understood what had happened. Peiyi, Madame Chang, Master Chao — all these people had plotted and acted to save him. Him, Rendi, who had sneered and scoffed, been rude and unfriendly, and who had tried so hard not to care about anyone or anything in this small, poor village. The night made a sobbing sound, and Rendi opened his mouth to speak, but the words he wished to say dried up as his eyes filled with tears. He blinked and swallowed, and finally said instead, "Where's the toad?"

Mr. Shan was kneeling forlornly over the pile of shattered dishes. His head was bowed as if in mourning, and Rendi felt as if he had swallowed a cold stone.

"Is... is the toad... is it all right?" Rendi choked out.

Mr. Shan looked over at Rendi, his eyes sorrowful like those of a hurt child. "No," he said.

CHAPTER
28

"Eerr—ripp." The toad gave a pitiful moan in Mr. Shan's hands.

Its belly still flashed green from the fireflies, but it was less noticeable in the brightly lit dining room. Rendi and his rescuers were sitting at a table, and all of them looked down sadly at the toad. The tea Rendi was drinking moistened his mouth, but his throat still felt tight and dry. The night murmured grief-filled noises. Rendi had never imagined a toad could mean so much to him.

Fang and Liu had not been careful during their terrified

flight out of the inn. The toad had tried to find refuge as the violent storm of plates and wine fell around it, but it could not escape Fang's and Liu's stomping, clumsy feet. Its back leg was a flattened, misshapen appendage.

"Can't we fix it?" MeiLan said softly.

Master Chao shook his head. "We'll have to cut the leg off," he said.

"Cut it off?" Peiyi said, horrified. "You can't cut it off!"

"We have to," Widow Yan told them. "It will be better for the toad."

"No!" Rendi said, shaking with a sudden fury. "You can't!"

Peiyi and Rendi stood side by side, as if soldiers preparing for battle. Rendi clenched his teeth, and his hands had formed into fists. Madame Chang led them away from the table.

"Sometimes the best decision is a painful one," she said to them. Peiyi looked back at the table and turned white. Rendi followed her gaze and saw Master Chao taking out his sharpest knife.

"*No!*" Rendi shouted, but Madame Chang stopped him before he could move. He tried to beat his fists at her, but she easily caught his hands and held them still. Her fingers, firm but gentle, were like cool water on a burn. The sky gave a sorrowful sigh.

"Rendi," Madame Chang said, her calm eyes bringing him to stillness, "sometimes the best decision is a painful one, but it is never one made out of anger."

Madame Chang sat him and Peiyi down, facing the windows. "Remember the story I told you of WangYi and his wife, the Moon Lady? How she took his pill of immortality and ended up on the moon? He only began to make good decisions when his anger left."

"Did he?" Peiyi said, but she was obviously still thinking about the toad.

"Yes," Madame Chang said.

THE STORY OF WANGYI'S DREAM

When WangYi's wife jumped to the moon and out of reach, WangYi was very angry. In his anger, he destroyed her possessions and married new wives and forbade anyone, even his children, to mention her. But his anger did not lessen, and he could not forget her. So he had pictures painted of her as a toad and told mocking stories of her being a grotesque creature that swallowed the moon. But his laughter held no joy, and every evening he cursed the moon.

His malice at the moon seemed only to fall back upon him, for it was his nights that became cursed. When he lay down to sleep at night, he felt as if his bed were made of hot coals. He could not rest. When he did sleep, he was plagued by nightmares. He was tormented with images of screaming people, dead animals, and bloody claws. Soon, his days and nights were filled with misery.

Finally, one night, during a fitful slumber, WangYi had a different dream. In his dream, an old man sat cross-legged in front of him, as if waiting. As WangYi approached, the old man stood up and began to walk away, gesturing WangYi to follow.

The old man guided WangYi across a flat stone land, completely empty except for two palaces side by side. The palaces were splendid and magnificent, with blue tiles that shone like the sunlit sky and walls as smooth as polished jade. Both palaces were exactly the same, except for the gold signs above the doorway. One sign said MISERY and the other said JOY.

The old man led WangYi into the palace marked MISERY. When they entered, they found themselves in a grand dining room where a lavish banquet was served. A rich, savory aroma filled the air from platters spilling over with food. The long table was hidden by all the delicious delicacies — bamboo shoots finely cut like plucked chrysanthemum petals, slices of duck with crisp amber skin, golden soup, and pieces of deep red pork shining as if lacquered — and the abundance was overwhelming.

However, the room was filled with shrieks of frustration and fury, and all the guests were gaunt and thin. They all had five-foot-long chopsticks, and because the chopsticks were so long, it was impossible for the food to reach their mouths. When they tried to eat using something other than the long chopsticks, the food disappeared — it was obvious that the food could be eaten only with the chopsticks. So the guests stretched and bent, trying to maneuver food from the long sticks but always failing. They screamed and raged, whimpered and wailed, all of them starving and taunted by the plentiful feast before them.

As WangYi watched with horror, the old man beckoned him out of the palace. Without a word, the old man led WangYi into the palace marked JOY. There, they again entered a grand dining room with the same abundant feast on the table. But instead of angry wails, the room was filled with laughter. The guests here also had five-foot-long chopsticks, but they were plump and healthy, joking and smiling. WangYi was puzzled. How could they eat with those long chopsticks? Then he noticed the difference.

The guests in this palace were feeding one another!

Before WangYi could shake his head in amazement, the old man beckoned to him again. WangYi followed the old man back out to the barren plain. In front of the palaces, the old man presented to him a pair of five-foot-long chopsticks. WangYi reached for the chopsticks, but they fell from his hand. He tried to pick them up from the ground, only to realize he had no fingers — only evil claws! They were the claws of a tiger!

WangYi awoke from his dream in a panic. As he sat in the darkness, he realized he was truly alone. His subjects despised him, his family feared him, and the only one who had loved him had left him. In the palace of joy, no one would feed him. And it looked as if he was destined to be unable to feed others as well. For the first time in a long time, WangYi began to weep.

But in the morning, WangYi was a changed man. He stopped roaring and yelling. He stopped his cruel and irrational actions and began to rule with justice and mercy. And he removed all the pictures of his wife as a toad.

With each good deed he did, with each wise decision he made, he felt as if the moon shone upon him, and he used his memory of his wife as his guide. He slowly regained his people's trust, but when they called him "WangYi the Great," he would only look wistfully up at the moon. As he grew older, the yearning to see his wife on the moon grew even stronger. He wished to see her once more before he died. So, one night, with hair more gray than black, WangYi climbed the tallest mountain.

When he reached the top, the moon was before him, large and glowing. He saw the figure of his wife. Just as had been rumored, she was no longer a toad but was now the pale, dark-eyed Moon Lady, more beautiful than he even remembered. She stared at him, but before he could say a word, she turned in fear and began to run.

"Don't go!" WangYi cried. "I've changed! I forgive you! Don't go!"

But she was gone, and WangYi fell onto his knees, heartbroken. He knew then how much he loved her. For the first time, he was glad that he had never taken the pill of immortality, for an eternal life of missing her was more than he could bear.

"Do you truly forgive her?" a voice said.

WangYi looked up and saw an old man sitting in front of him cross-legged, a book in his lap. The old man from his dream!

WangYi nodded, unable to speak.

"Good," the old man said. "For you are destined to be together."

The old man knocked his walking stick against the stone ground. Immediately, a green vine sprouted, twisting upward. Heart-shaped leaves budded and opened, and then a berry, so brilliant it seemed made of fire, grew. A great golden bird with a crimson crown flew down from the sky, plucked the berry with its beak, and brought it to WangYi.

"Eat the berry," the old man said. "Not only will it grant you immortality, it will protect you from the heat of the sun."

"Why do I need protection?" WangYi asked, holding the berry in his hand.

"Because you will live there," the old man said. "You will live in the Palace of the Sun while your wife lives in the Palace of the Moon."

"Not together?" WangYi said.

"No," the old man said, and looked at him deliberately. "WangYi, you are like the power that has marked you. Great but easily spoiled and in need of balance. You will rule at the Palace of the Sun, and if you rule wisely and well, the Celestial Rooster will fly you to the moon and back every twenty-nine days."

And so it was. WangYi and his wife reconciled, and WangYi rules on the Sun, raising it in the sky during the day and lowering it at night. Because he does this faithfully, he is allowed to fly to see his wife for one night every twenty-nine days. On the night he arrives, the moon is full and bright, as the Moon Lady is happy and joyous. But after he leaves, she worries that he may again lapse into bad behavior and will not be able to visit, so the moon wanes and fades.

"But there's no moon now," Peiyi said, "and he's still doing his job. The sun rises every day."

"Yes," Madame Chang said. "He is doing his job faithfully. The missing moon is not WangYi's fault. He is continuing his job, waiting for when he can visit her."

"Is that why it's so hot out?" Peiyi asked. "Is WangYi working extra hard because he wants to prove he's worthy to visit his wife? But if the moon is missing, where will he visit her?"

"Maybe she is on the sun with him," Rendi said.

"No," Peiyi scoffed. "She can't go to the sun — she didn't eat that berry. What happened to her when the moon disappeared?"

"She probably fell into the Starry River of the Sky," Rendi said. "She could have even fallen through the sky and landed on the earth. She could be anywhere! The moon could be anywhere!"

"Yes," Peiyi said, now turning to Madame Chang. "Where is the moon? And where is the Moon Lady?"

What she might have answered was lost, for at that moment, there was a clatter behind them.

"We are finished," MeiLan called as Master Chao and Widow Yan collected knives and other implements from the table. Rendi, Peiyi, and Madame Chang rushed back to Mr. Shan and the toad.

"Is it all right?" Rendi asked, his throat returning to dryness.

Mr. Shan held out the toad. The deformed, crushed leg was gone, and a cloth bandage was wrapped around the toad's body. The night sighed again, but the toad no longer made anguished moans. It looked up with large eyes.

"Three-legged toad," Mr. Shan said.

CHAPTER
29

After going to bed late, Peiyi, Rendi, and Master Chao overslept the next morning. However, the duke and his men were still sound asleep when they got up, which gave them plenty of time to remove all traces of the night's adventure. Peiyi and Rendi swept and scoured Fang and Liu's room and gave it a good airing, for the odor of the fermented tofu had not been improved by a night in the warm air. They threw Fang's and Liu's coats into the ragbag, and they buried the items found in Fang's small bag (matches, an evil-looking knife, and other various unpleasant-looking items) in the yard.

"Rendi," Peiyi said as they patted the earth on top of Fang's buried items, "why did those men kidnap you? Did they think you were going to warn the duke about them?"

"No," Rendi said.

"Then why?" Peiyi pressed.

Rendi hesitated. Hundreds of words came to his head, but none came out of his mouth.

"Fine, if you don't want to tell me," Peiyi said, mistaking his silence. She ran back into the inn, obviously hurt.

"No, wait!" Rendi said, but it was too late. The back door had closed. Rendi sighed. Should he go after her? Rendi shrugged and followed.

But there wasn't an opportunity to talk to Peiyi, as the dining room was full of activity. Duke Zhe and his men had finally woken up and were demanding breakfast, even though it was lunchtime. Before Rendi could say a word, both he and Peiyi were hopping from table to table, and Master Chao was wiping his brow.

The duke and his men did not laugh or make jokes the way they had the evening — had it only been an evening? — before. They were heavy-eyed and gruff, and the duke was petulant, often closing his eyes in irritation and touching his temple with his fingers. They were most likely still feeling the effects of the drugged wine. Soon and without enjoyment, they finished eating, and Rendi was sent to get the horses.

As Rendi put the blankets on the horses, he looked at his hands. "Those aren't the hands of a rich boy," Fang had said. When Rendi first arrived at the inn, they had been as soft and white as freshly steamed rice. Now they were sunburned and scarred.

But they could still feel the richness of cloth. The silk of the horse blankets was cool and smooth against his skin, and the material was so fine that it did not catch even on the roughness of his fingers. For one brief moment, Rendi brushed his face against it, closing his eyes.

Rendi brought the horses to the duke's men, who harnessed some to the carriages and readied others for riding. The duke idly waited, as did Peiyi and Master Chao —

who stood to give their farewell salute. Rendi took a deep breath and approached the duke.

"Excuse me, honorable duke?" Rendi bowed. He felt the eyes of Peiyi and Master Chao on him.

"Yes, boy?" the duke said with a slight annoyed edge to his voice.

"The boy you are looking for, Magistrate Tiger's son..." Rendi began. He could feel Peiyi edging closer, listening curiously.

"Magistrate Wang!" the duke said shortly. "I was imprudent to disclose a servant's nickname for him. His name is Magistrate Wang."

"Magistrate Wang's son...you're looking for him?" Rendi began to stutter with nervousness. "He...I... where..."

"Yes, yes," the duke said impatiently, and he motioned a direction with his arm. "We're going south to the City of Far Remote. I believe kidnappers have brought him there."

"You won't find him at the City of Far Remote," Rendi stammered. From the corners of his eyes, he saw Peiyi frowning at him with puzzlement.

"I think I will," the duke said. "I have the fastest horses of the land, as fast as the emperor's. We can catch up with the kidnappers."

"But there are no kidnappers..." Rendi tried again, his face flushing. The duke's men had finished attaching the horses to the carriages and were opening a door for the duke to enter.

"Don't worry," the duke said, stepping into his carriage. He gave Rendi a patronizing smile. "I have influence in ways you cannot conceive."

"But... but..." Rendi said, panicked, and then had to shout as the carriage began to move. "Magistrate Wang's son isn't in the city!"

"We'll be fine!" the duke called from his window. He waved with a languid motion. "My men are very skilled. We are all quite capable!"

Rendi could say nothing else as the carriages and horses raced off. Too bewildered to join Peiyi and Master Chao in their customary farewell salute, Rendi simply stared. A cloud of dust, like the breath of an earth dragon, rose in the air. As it hid the carriages from view, Rendi felt a strange mixture of relief and disappointment.

CHAPTER
30

It was already late in the day when Rendi, Peiyi, and Master Chao turned back to the inn. They were quickly at work again, rushing to finish their regular chores. It was only as Madame Chang and Mr. Shan sat down to dinner when they were able to rest.

But instead of resting, Rendi stood.

"Madame Chang," Rendi said, "I have a story I would like to tell."

Peiyi looked at him with the same curious expression

she had given him all day, but Madame Chang did not look surprised. She nodded, and Rendi began.

 # THE STORY OF MAGISTRATE TIGER'S SON

Magistrate Tiger was very proud of the prizes he received from the emperor. He filled the *gang* with water and goldfish, displaying it prominently in his formal chamber. Directly above it, on a high shelf, he exhibited the blue-and-white rice bowl on its gold stand. Whenever he had visitors, he would retell how he had answered the emperor's impossible questions, impressing all with his wisdom.

Of course, Magistrate Tiger's son would scowl during these narratives, which seemed to grow grander and more extraordinary each time. "He didn't even thank us for giving him the answers," the boy said to his sister, his lower lip jutting out. "The bowl and *gang* are really ours."

That feeling did not lessen over time. One day, even though he was forbidden to go into his father's formal chamber, he stood at the doorway and looked in with greedy eyes. The gold stand of the rice bowl glinted in the light. It seemed to signal to him. "I just want to see them," he said to himself as he stepped into the room.

He walked softly to the huge *gang*. It was taller than he and wider, a bit like the vats they made wine in. But, of course, this was no plain earthenware tub. The thin, decorated porcelain was cold and smooth to his fingers, like a piece of polished jade. The boy climbed onto the shelf and looked into the *gang*. A dozen orange fish flickered in the water, like wavering flames. His reflection looked back at him with eyes full of secrets, and, above him, the gold flashed.

The boy looked up and saw the blue-and-white rice bowl, sitting silently on the gold stand. His fingers could only barely touch the bottom of the stand. He scaled the shelves, mounting the ledge above the *gang*. Could he reach the bowl? Yes!

"What are you doing?" a voice said behind him.

The boy spun around in surprise to see his sister

staring at him, openmouthed. But before he could say a word, the precious rice bowl fell from his fingers. He frantically grabbed at it, leaning and tilting, his feet slipping and…*splash*! He fell right into the *gang*!

Cold, shocking water slapped him and filled his mouth and eyes. His elbows and hands banged against the slippery walls of the *gang*, but he couldn't find the edge. There was not enough room to swim, and when the bottom of the *gang* seemed to have vanished, he began to panic. He felt as if invisible arms had seized him. He writhed and struggled, but the heavy water pressed into him, holding him. His lungs began to burn, a hot, dry, suffocating burn. He dimly heard his sister's scream. Her small hands could not reach him, and her efforts to push the heavy *gang* over were futile. She would have to get help, he thought as blackness began to overtake him. But it would be too late. He was drowning, drowning…

Crack! Suddenly, water rushed away from his face, and he was on the floor, coughing and choking. His sister was by his side, lifting his head as he wheezed and panted for air. Sweet, delicious air! The darkness in his eyes began to fade, and he saw what had happened.

Unable to reach him, unable to overturn the *gang*, and afraid to run for help, his sister had grabbed an inkstone from the table and had smashed it into the *gang*. The delicate porcelain had cracked like an eggshell, and she'd broken a hole in it to free him. She was so smart! He looked at her with gratitude.

"*What has happened?!*" a roar echoed through the room, and both children gasped. Their father!

Magistrate Tiger's sharp eyes scanned everything — the bedraggled boy coughing on the floor, the white-faced girl, and the fallen rice bowl next to the boy. He saw the pool of water, the dying fish, and then the broken shards of his precious, prized *gang*.

"MY...*GANG*...MY..." he stuttered, and his roars slowly turned to a thunderous wail as he rushed to the broken *gang*, grabbing pieces of it in disbelief. "*Broken!*"

"I did it," the girl said, her voice quavering.

"To save me!" the boy said quickly. "I was drowning..."

"I DON'T CARE!" Magistrate Tiger shouted, his bellows a mixture of anguish and anger. "MY *GANG*! GIVEN BY THE EMPEROR...!"

"We're sorry!" the girl whispered, beginning to sob.

"SORRY? ONLY SORRY? YOU USELESS WORMS!" Magistrate Tiger's fury began to explode like a thousand bursting firecrackers as he clutched at the shards of the broken *gang*. "THESE PIECES ARE WORTH MORE THAN YOU!"

The girl trembled like a kite caught in a typhoon, but the boy was strangely still, his eyes darkening. It was as if a smoldering red coal had finally burst into flames inside him. His father had seen him half drowned on the floor, yet he had run first to the broken *gang*. Black bitterness gripped the boy, and a rage that matched his father's filled him. His mother had lied! His sister had lied! Everyone had lied! His father did not roar and lie and cheat for him. His father did not care about him! In fact, he cared more about the shattered *gang*. Suddenly, he hated all of them. He hated everything. He hated his mother, his sister, his father, his home. He wished everything would disappear. He wished he could disappear.

And with that thought, the boy scooped up the wet but unharmed rice bowl and stood. Without another word, he walked out of the room, leaving the roars and sobs behind.

"That's not the end, is it?" Peiyi asked.

Rendi shrugged. Like the room, the sky was quiet and waiting. It was sunset, and even though the sun had gone down beyond the horizon, there was still light.

"What else happened?" Peiyi persisted. "What did the boy do?"

Rendi opened his mouth, but no words would form.

"He ran away, didn't he?" Madame Chang said gently. "He ran away, unable to stay in a house where he was loved less than a piece of porcelain."

Rendi could say nothing, and a myriad of pinks and oranges filled the sky.

"He probably went far with the money in his pockets,"

Madame Chang mused. "But eventually, his money would run out."

Again, Rendi could make no sound. The pink sky was turning purple, and a rose-gold glow spilled into the room.

"Maybe he even sold his fine clothes and stowed away on carts and caravans, getting as far as he could, until he was poor and ragged and had nothing left," Madame Chang said. "Except, perhaps, the good fortune to find someone willing to take him in as a chore boy."

Tears welled in Rendi's eyes, and finally a noise formed in his throat. But it was a sob, the same sound of sorrow he heard so often in the wind. His eyes blurred as the tears began to flow freely, so he did not see Peiyi, Master Chao, and the others draw near to comfort him.

But he felt them all.

CHAPTER
31

That night, Rendi lay awake in his bed. He thought about Fang and Liu, the duke, and all that had happened. Was his father really looking for him? He was unsure how that made him feel. He stared out into the black sky while the wind moaned again.

The cries grew louder in Rendi's ears. What was crying like that? And for the first time, Rendi wondered why. Was the person in pain? Why didn't anyone help him?

But Madame Chang said she heard the cries only

faintly, and no one else seemed to hear them at all. Did Mr. Shan? Rendi remembered Mr. Shan's back straightening stiffly when the groans blew in. Maybe Mr. Shan heard them too. But did no one hear them the way he did? The plaintive call, beckoning and begging?

He sat up. Whoever was crying had been doing so for weeks and weeks! Maybe no one had helped because Rendi was the only one who could really hear it. A sudden shame filled him. Ever since he started hearing the cries, all he had thought about was himself, never about who was suffering or how he could help.

Well, he would find out and help now, Rendi thought with determination. It was his turn to save someone. He stood up and took the plain cloth bag from his drawer, the same one he had packed so long ago. Now he emptied it of his belongings and started to repack. What did one bring for something like this? he thought. Extra clothes? Cloth for bandages? A knife? Maybe the person was crying out of hunger. Food, then, and a jug of wine.

Rendi tiptoed to the kitchen, filling his bag with anything he thought might be helpful, his bag a bit unwieldy as he slung it over his shoulders. Then he took a lantern heavy with oil and crept out of the inn.

The dark night was full of sad groans, and for a moment, Rendi felt as if they were coming from the empty sky above. Slowly, he located the direction of the moans. Yet as he lit the lantern, he gulped.

The moans were coming from across the Stone Pancake! That rock that stretched for miles and miles. He would be lost in no time out there.

The groans came again, and Rendi took a deep breath. Maybe that was why the person was crying. Maybe someone was lost out there on the stone plain! Well, if he was going to save them, he had to go but not get lost himself. "I just have to mark my way," he said, "so I can find my way back."

He swung the lantern around the yard, trying to find something to help him. The light shone on a pile of empty snail shells — garbage from Master Chao's new dishes. They were dry from being in the daytime sun, and there were a lot of them. "I'll use those," Rendi whispered, filling his pockets.

The breeze carried another sad whimper, and Rendi

stepped onto the flat stone. He raised the lantern and looked at the endless blackness in front of him. He dropped a snail shell, listened, and walked forward. He took one step after another, occasionally dropping a snail shell, until he was a small pinprick of light, like a bright star in the darkness.

CHAPTER
32

Rendi felt as if he had been walking for miles. As his pockets began to lighten, he dropped snail shells less frequently, and he began to worry that he would not have enough. But just when he ran out, something other than flat stone and black sky formed in the landscape. A large, tall shadow of a tree reached into the Starry River like an arm beckoning. As Rendi walked closer, he was also able to see a stone bridge that extended over a lake, both almost invisible in the darkness.

The lantern created a circle of light around Rendi as he walked over the bridge. When he saw his reflection in the still water, he felt as if he were walking over the night sky, for there seemed no difference between the two. The moans grew stronger and stronger with each step he took, so he knew he was going in the right direction.

He stepped off the bridge onto grassy ground. The weeds, getting their water from the lake, were soft under his feet, so different from the dried, scorched plants in the village. With his lantern held high, Rendi saw a low hilly area before him.

The groans grew even louder, and Rendi frowned. It seemed as if the cries were coming from inside one of the hills!

Stretching the light out in front of him, Rendi peered into the darkness. One of the hills appeared to have a large black opening. Was there a cave in that hill? He walked closer, and words came back to his ears. "*An ancient dark hole in one of the hills*," Madame Chang had said in her stories. "*A dark hole, like a cave.*"

Rendi swung around, the lantern swaying. It was just like the place Madame Chang had described. A lake. A tall tree. An ancient cave. All that was missing was the mountain. As Rendi stood in front of the opening, he gulped. Did this mean the White Tiger lived in there? But the White Tiger was gone now. Was it a different vicious tiger that had been moaning all this time?

Another groan resonated from the darkness in front of him. The groan was sad and mournful, like a temple bell at a funeral. But there was also something else in the sound. There was yearning, a longing in it that was an echo of something deep inside Rendi's own chest and what made him finally enter.

"Hello?" Rendi called. His voice was thin, and it faded into the endless blackness. In the cave, the air was cool, and the earth was soft on his feet. "Hello?"

Another moan blew at him, and Rendi raised his lantern even higher. There was something in front of him. Something very large. He could make out a huge form — bigger than a horse but, strangely, shapeless. It was glowing with an eerie, soft, faint green light. What was it?

Rendi took slow, careful steps forward, the light shaking from the trembling lantern.

Suddenly, from the strange mass, two enormous eyes blinked open. Like two round melons, they bulged and stared right at Rendi. They were the eyes of a monstrous toad!

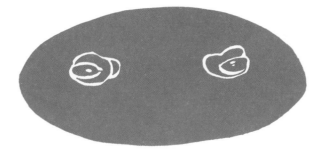

CHAPTER

33

Rendi shrieked and ran back the way he had come, his heart thundering louder than his feet on the ground. His fear overwhelmed any thoughts. Was it the real Noxious Toad? Would it breathe on him with its poisonous vapor? Rendi burst out of the hill, gasping and panting.

The cool breeze from the lake blew over him, calming him like a gentle touch. The light from his lantern flickered over the water, making twinkling stars in the rippling waves. The tranquil scene soothed him, and as he caught his breath, another moan came from the hill. It did not seem malicious. It seemed sad. And then Rendi remembered the eyes — those eyes of the monstrous toad were full of pain and sorrow. They were, in fact, much like the eyes of Mr. Shan's toad when it became three-legged, Rendi thought with a pang.

What if that giant toad wasn't the Noxious Toad? Rendi thought, his mind racing. What if... what if it was WangYi's wife? What if Madame Chang was wrong and WangYi's wife had never turned back into a woman? What if she had stayed a toad? And with the moon missing, she was stuck here on earth, hiding in this hill?

A dim light began to spill out of the hill. The toad had followed him! But it was moving so slowly, Rendi could easily run and disappear from sight by the time the toad exited. Rendi looked at the bridge but stood still and waited.

The toad finally emerged, its greenish glow lighting the surroundings as if it were a giant, misshapen lantern. The toad was so large that Rendi's head just reached the top of its bulbous leg, and its warty skin was like weathered, rotting leather. Rendi quaked again at its monstrous ugliness, but the toad gave another pathetic moan of pain, and Rendi's pity drove away his fear.

The toad did not look well. The odd green glow was coming from its bloated belly and made it look wan and sickly. No wonder the toad had moved so slowly. It continued to hold its stomach with both of its front legs and moaned.

Rendi wondered if it had swallowed fireflies like Mr. Shan's toad had. It must have had to swallow a lot, Rendi thought, surveying the size of the toad's swollen belly. But that would explain why it had a stomachache, at least.

Rendi felt the weight of the bag on his shoulders. Would the wine make the toad feel better? He took out the jug.

"Maybe this will help your stomach," Rendi said, holding out the wine. His words felt clumsy and out of place in the still night. "Do you want to try it?"

The toad's eyelids lifted halfway, and its eyes, as black as watermelon seeds, looked at the jug.

"It's Son Wine," Rendi said. "It's good. I should know. My father invented it."

The toad made a questioning noise, and Rendi, to fill the silence and perhaps out of habit, began to tell the story.

THE STORY OF SON WINE

When my mother was with child for the first time, my father, the magistrate, was overjoyed. "The blood of the greatest ruler and hero will be passed on," he declared triumphantly. "My blood will continue in my son."

Accordingly, he planned a grand feast for when the baby was to be born. He told his servants to fatten a pig, to make eighty-eight jars of the finest rice wine, and to prepare for the greatest festivities the township had ever seen. He laughed and joked boisterously, accepting congratulations as if his wife had already given birth. My mother worried, but in my father's mind, a son already existed. His imagination had lost all boundaries, and my father pictured a son gifted with as much strength, bravery, and cleverness as an immortal. *My son will become king,* he thought with grand contentment, *and then his son will become emperor, and we will rule again!*

So when a daughter was born, my father was

devastated. When the midwives told him that my mother had given birth to a girl, his face blackened like burned wood, and he stormed out of the room without even glancing at the baby. "A daughter!" he said bitterly.

My father was angry at the baby girl, as if she had somehow stolen the son he was expecting. In a rage, he turned all the guests from his door and ordered the banquet feast to be thrown to the pigs and the jars of wine buried. If anyone offered him a word of congratulations, he scowled and ordered them from his sight.

For the next year, my mother and the servants kept the baby out of his way as much as possible. My father's anger slowly lessened, but the resentment remained. When my mother told him they were expecting another child, he only replied, "Will it be another girl, like the last one?"

This time, my father did not prepare a banquet or brew wine or boast. He felt humiliated from before, and he did not even dare to dream about a son this time.

But when the baby was born, it was me, a boy! My father's wish for a son was fulfilled!

My father was overwhelmed with joy and pride. He strutted and trumpeted like a rooster, inviting all the officials and people of his township to what he promised would be a splendid celebration.

However, since my father had made no preparations ahead of time, there was now a great rush. Servants ran from peddler to grocer all over the city; the pig — which was now extremely fat — was quickly butchered; and his chefs worked without sleeping. Throughout the night, they were coloring red eggs until their hands and arms were dyed as well, and when the rooster crowed in the morning, the chefs were stewing, roasting, and boiling so quickly that the steam became as thick as smoke. They fried golden sesame balls as round as plums and cut ginger into delicate, paper-thin slices so that it looked like flower petals on a plate. Platters of dark honey-colored pork were garnished with jade-green lettuce, and white dumplings floated in bowls of sweet soup like clouds. The servants proudly placed the food on the table.

"But where is the wine?" my father demanded. "I cannot hold a celebration without wine! Get the wine!"

The servants retreated and looked at one another blankly. They could not make wine in such a short amount of time. What could they do?

Finally, a servant remembered something. "There are the eighty-eight jars of wine that we buried when the magistrate's daughter was born," he said. "We can dig them up!"

So they did. When my father readied to open the doors of his home, it was a glorious feast. It was his proudest moment. When I, his son, was revealed, my father's delight seemed to transform him. In his happiness, kind words and compliments flowed from him like a spring river. He himself brought my mother the bowl of strengthening ginger soup and even gently patted my sister's head. The birth of a son had, at least for the day, turned the old bitterness sweet.

Which was much like the wine that was served. After being buried in the ground so long, the wine had a different scent and taste. It was fragrant and pure, and all the guests agreed it was delicious.

"What kind of wine is this?" an official asked my

father. "I've never tasted wine quite like this before. How did you brew it?"

"It is Son Wine," my father said after a pause, "to celebrate my son! The servants can tell you how it was made."

"And so Son Wine, this wine, was created," Rendi said. "I was the son the wine honored, but I always thought it should be called Daughter Wine because it was made when my sister was born. I always felt it wasn't fair that my father didn't celebrate her. She's smarter than me, and braver too."

Rendi looked off into the far distance, past where the light of his lantern shone. The giant toad made no sound.

"When I said that to my mother and sister," Rendi continued, "they told me it didn't matter. They said because I was born, our father stopped hating my sister for not being a boy and resenting my mother for not having a son. My sister even said that when I was born it made everything right and happy, so I deserved the celebration because everyone loved me so..."

Rendi's voice broke off. He stopped speaking and shook his head, trying to forget his own words. But then he looked up at the toad, and their eyes met.

And suddenly, in that moment, Rendi's secret wish was revealed, a wish he didn't even know he had. Because when Rendi looked into the toad's eyes, he knew why the toad cried. *The toad wished to go home.* And Rendi could hear those cries because he did too.

All this time he had tried to forget his past, hating when he remembered. He had told himself he never wanted to go back, but one look into the eyes of this toad, and he knew that was not the truth. He missed his sister and he missed his mother and he even missed his father. He missed his home.

His eyes mirrored the toad's, and all filled with tears. They were both missing their homes, just as WangYi was missing his wife and like the sky was missing the moon.

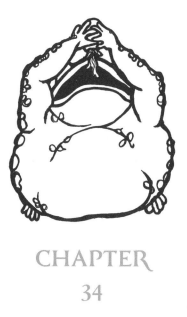

CHAPTER
34

For a long moment, the toad and the boy stared at each other with silent understanding. Then the toad gave a painful groan and clutched at its bulging belly once again. The strange green glow grew brighter. Rendi looked at it with pity, all fear and disgust gone.

"Try the wine," Rendi urged, holding the jug with both hands. "It can't hurt."

The toad hesitated but finally took the wine, its large hands almost covering the jar entirely. With a swift motion, the toad raised and turned the jug upside down above its head. The jug emptied quickly, the wine pouring like a waterfall into the waiting black half circle of the toad's open mouth. The toad's eyes closed, looking like two enormous loganberries slit with black lines, as it swallowed with a satisfied gulp.

The toad dropped the jug to the ground with a soft thud.

"Do you feel better?" Rendi asked.

The toad's eyes reopened and looked at Rendi as if dazed. The light from the toad's belly dimmed slightly as it gurgled a churning noise, much like the bubbling of soup.

"Are...are you all right?" Rendi asked, alarmed.

The wine seemed to be having an unusual effect on the toad. It was swaying slightly from side to side, its arms no longer clutching its stomach but hanging limply. Its eyes bulged as if they were going to explode.

Then, as Rendi stared in horror, the toad's mouth expanded like the opening of a tunnel. The toad drew in a deep breath, and Rendi could feel the air around him being sucked away as...

"BURPPPPPP!!!!!!"

The toad gave a belch that echoed across the hills, blowing Rendi's hair and making a cresting wave in the water. Rendi staggered as the air, smelling of wine and wetness, pushed him backward. But, turning his head, he saw that it was not just air that the toad expelled. Its enormous mouth widened, and something round and shining fell to the earth.

The glimmering ball rolled past Rendi's feet, and he could not look away from it. Was it a dragon's pearl? It was so white and perfectly round, revolving on the ground like a bamboo yo-yo on a string.

But with every turn, it grew larger and larger, bigger than any dragon's pearl Rendi had ever heard of. It also grew brighter as the soft grass rubbed off any slime from the toad, and it began to gleam as if it were lit from within. When the ball finally stopped rolling, it was taller than Master Chao and the most beautiful thing Rendi had ever seen. Smoother than the finest jade, more luminous than the finest pearl, it was radiant. It shone with a pure light that illuminated everything with a silver shimmering frost. Rendi could scarcely breathe.

"The moon!" he whispered. It could not be anything else. *The toad has burped up the moon*, Rendi thought in a daze. He turned to look at the toad.

It was gone.

CHAPTER
35

Where the toad had been, a person was stretched on the ground. But it was not a woman, not the Moon Lady, but a man. He was a young man and completely naked, the tall grass bending over him like a sheltering caress.

"Hello?" Rendi said, just as he had when he entered the cave.

The man turned his head and looked at Rendi. As if weighed down by air, he slowly sat up and rubbed his face with his hands. Then he stared at his hands as if mesmerized. The light of the moon made his face clearly visible, and it was strangely familiar. Where had Rendi seen those eyes before? That mouth? That forehead?

"Jiming?" Rendi asked in a voice that was barely above a whisper.

The man's eyes jerked back to Rendi, and his face flashed a grin. There was no doubt now. That was Peiyi's smile! This man had to be her brother. He had to be Jiming.

The man began to laugh, a sound of pure joy and gratitude. He threw up both of his arms and sprang into the air with such a great jump that Rendi suspected not everything about being a toad had left him.

"I am Jiming!" the man whooped. He began to run and leap, like a horse feeling freedom for the first time. The moon bathed his naked figure in light as his fingers reached to touch the stars, his hair streaming. "I am *not* a toad!" he hollered, triumphant. "I am Jiming!"

Rendi couldn't help laughing. He fell to the ground, spasms of laughter clenching his stomach. As he fell, he felt his bag underneath him. He had clothes! Rendi remembered. And he had food.

"Jiming! Jiming!" Rendi called as the man's dance in the night slowed. "Do you want some pants?"

The pants did not fit well, barely falling below Jiming's knees. But Jiming cheerfully squeezed into them, removing the drawstring completely. He sat down in the grass across from Rendi, accepting the cold rice balls he offered. The moon enveloped them in its soft, tranquil light.

"So who are you?" Jiming asked. "Other than a boy who brings wine to toads at night."

"I'm Rendi. I'm the chore boy at your father's inn," Rendi said. Jiming stiffened, and Rendi hurried on. "But what happened to you? Where have you been? How did you become a toad?"

Jiming stared out at the lake in front of him. "It seems a dream now," he said.

THE STORY OF JIMING'S TRANSFORMATION

My father and I had an argument. It was a very bad one, the worst we had ever had. We said terrible things to each other, and when I slammed the door behind me, I vowed never to return.

I was so angry that I did not realize for some time that I had been stomping across the Stone Pancake, going farther than I had ever gone before. When I did realize it, I did not care. I wanted to get lost. I wanted to never be able to find my way back to the inn or my father ever again.

When I passed the stone plain, I barely saw the bridge over the lake, and I definitely did not see the figure crossing it while reading a book. I stormed onto the bridge, violently colliding with the person. He and his bag were knocked to the ground and his book flew into the water, causing a splash so great that I felt the water splatter on my face. It was old Mr. Shan, and he jumped up and looked over the edge of the bridge with a noise of despair. He swung back toward me, his black eyes flashing.

"Jiming!" Mr. Shan said. "If you aren't careful, your anger will burn you up inside!"

I grunted an apology and continued my outraged march. But his words began to repeat over and over again with my stamping feet. *Your anger will burn. Your anger will burn.* And, then, my anger *was* burning. Inside, I felt as if there were a fire inside me, flaming and smoldering.

The bridge ended, and I went to the edge of the lake. The water was so still and black that it melted into the sky, and there were twin moons in the darkness. One moon was like a white jade plate floating in front of me. However, the burning was becoming unbearable. I did not gaze long. Instead, I kneeled down and began to drink.

I drank and drank, trying to extinguish the fire I felt inside. I watched the reflection of the moon siphon away as I gulped and swallowed. Then, all of a sudden, without any warning, I felt as if I was going to burst. I fell back, bloated and swollen, and threw off my clothes, which were choking me. As I struggled with my pants, I was horrified to see that my feet had puffed out and were webbed. The skin on my arms and legs had become thick and rough and spotted. But the worst was my stomach. It was grotesquely bulging, glowing, and it ached — a pressing pain that left me gasping.

I crawled back to the lake's edge and recoiled at what I saw. My ballooned stomach cast the light for me to see that I had become a monstrous toad. I shrank back, afraid of my own image. The pain in my stomach as well as my huge size forced me to move slowly, but I pulled myself away — trying to get as far from my reflection as possible.

Finally, I found myself in a tunnel-like cave in a hill, and there I stayed. In my new toad shape, the daylight sun and heat were agonizing, and my new home was cool and dark. Not that I was ever comfortable. During the day, the pain in my stomach was a tender, dull ache. But as night fell, it would begin to throb and grow, and I could only moan and cry in helpless, agonizing pain. And that was how I lived until you came.

"You must have swallowed the moon when you drank from the lake! I wonder why it turned you into a toad," Rendi said. He thought about Madame Chang's story. Was the moon a pill of immortality too? "Anyway, that's why I always heard those groans at night!"

"It was me," Jiming said with a wry expression on his face. "I was miserable! Every night I wished I had never left home."

"Well, now you can go back!" Rendi said, grinning.

Jiming hesitated, his eyes cast downward.

"I don't know," Jiming said in a low voice.

"What do you mean?" Rendi asked, astounded. "Everyone wants you to come back! Your father and Widow Yan aren't fighting anymore, did you know? You can marry MeiLan now."

Jiming's face flushed at the mention of MeiLan's name.

"Maybe MeiLan could meet me here," Jiming said. "You could give her a message, and we could go away somewhere..."

"Go away somewhere? But you want to go home!" Rendi said, remembering the truth in the toad's eyes. He almost stood up in dismay. "What about Peiyi? What about your father? What about you?"

"It's not that simple," Jiming said. "I can't... I can't just forgive everything and go back home!"

"But that's what you want!" Rendi said in disbelief. "If you don't forgive your father, you're the one who suffers!"

Then Rendi fell silent, an uncomfortable realization coming over him. He was glad when Jiming responded.

"Maybe you're right," Jiming said, and he looked over at the moon. It was a shining, perfect pearl in the silk darkness of the night. "And I suppose the Village of Clear Sky wants its moon back too."

CHAPTER
36

"It's like trying to lift a mountain," Jiming said, gasping.

Both Rendi and Jiming had been straining every muscle to lift the moon, but it stayed rooted firmly to the ground. The moon was incredibly heavy.

Jiming glanced at the flat stone plain in the distance with a crooked smile. "It can't be impossible to move, though."

Rendi shrugged. Jiming was now fully dressed in his own clothes. They had found them after a quick search by the lake, and after shaking out a few frogs and crickets, saw that they were none the worse for wear. Straining and pushing the moon, Jiming reminded Rendi of Master Chao on the day he had arrived at the Village of Clear Sky when they moved that *gang* of wine…

"Jiming! I know how we can move the moon!" Rendi said. "We have to roll it!"

And Rendi was right. The moon could not be lifted, but it could be rolled.

It was not easily rolled, however. The smooth surface was slippery, and the weight made it difficult to push. For all its round symmetry, rolling the moon was a slow procedure. Inch by inch, Rendi and Jiming rolled the moon to the bridge.

When they were halfway across the bridge, they heard faint calls from the stone plain.

"Rendi!" the voices were calling. "Rendi!"

That's Peiyi's voice, Rendi thought. *And Madame Chang's and Widow Yan's.* They must have been worried and gone looking for him, Rendi realized. He looked at the figures standing by the tall tree, their lanterns drooping as they gazed toward him. The moon cast a pure light, and Rendi, perhaps for the first time, saw them clearly. There was Master Chao, full of pride yet good-hearted, and Peiyi, fearless yet vulnerable. There were Widow Yan and MeiLan, weighed down by worries but unbroken, and Madame Chang and Mr. Shan, staring with soft expressions of homecoming. Their kindness and caring seemed to reach for him, and the moon began to roll as if pulled by a silver ribbon.

Crrriiick! Suddenly, there was sickening crack, and the waiting faces changed to expressions of horror.

"The bridge!" Jiming gasped. "It's not strong enough for the moon! The bridge is breaking!"

Criickkk! Criiick! Rendi and Jiming, their hands on the moon, stood frozen. *Criiiiiick!* The bridge gave a slow, stomach-turning groan, and Peiyi screamed.

"*Mr. Shan!*" Madame Chang said. It was not a statement or a question. It was an order. The walking stick clattered to the ground, and with long strides, moving faster than Rendi ever could have imagined, Mr. Shan flew toward them. From his pocket, the three-legged toad gave a miraculous jump and was quickly scooped up by Madame Chang. And then Mr. Shan leaped into the lake.

The groaning of the bridge stopped.

"Go ahead, Rendi," Mr. Shan's voice said from below him. Was Mr. Shan under the bridge?

"What?" Rendi said.

"He's holding up the bridge!" Peiyi shouted from the lake's edge. She raised both of her arms in the air, imitating Mr. Shan's posture. Beside her, Master Chao beckoned madly. "Hurry up!"

Rendi and Jiming pushed with renewed effort. The moon rolled faster, as if it were being drawn to the waiting figures. Rendi could hear Peiyi's excited babble before the moon even reached the end of the bridge.

"We thought those men might have come back to kidnap you," she was saying. "I saw the snail shells, and I thought maybe you left them as a trail for us! And so we followed it. Who's that with you? How did you find the moon? Why did you..."

The moon rolled onto the grass, and Jiming took a step out from behind it.

"Jiming!!!" Peiyi shrieked. Figures flew like swooping birds as all, even MeiLan, who forgot about maidenly modesty in her joy, rushed to hug and squeeze and cry over Jiming. Rendi grinned but stood back. Perhaps that

is why he was the only one who heard the loud splash in the water.

When Rendi turned to look, he saw Mr. Shan bursting through the lake surface, drops of silver water flung into the air like thrown stars. Mr. Shan raised his hands overhead in a triumphant gesture, and Rendi saw he was holding a large book dripping with water.

"I found it!" Mr. Shan said.

CHAPTER
37

"I don't understand about the moon," Peiyi said, gently stroking its smooth surface with a single finger. "It's very beautiful and it is big. But it isn't big enough for WangYi's wife to live on. Isn't she supposed to have a palace on it?"

"That's because the moon has fallen from the sky," Madame Chang said. She was hovering around it like a white-winged moth. "The moon is like a closed flower now. When it enters the Starry River, it expands and a palace of water jade and pearl grows."

"Well, how do we get the moon back into the sky?" Jiming said. "I think that's the problem."

"Maybe if we roll it into the lake..." Rendi started.

"No," Mr. Shan said. He was dripping wet, but he did not seem to notice. He held his book in his arms as if it were a newborn child and said, "The sky cannot reflect the lake. The moon must be returned to the sky."

"It's very late," Master Chao cut in. "I think we will not be able to return the moon tonight."

"Yes," Widow Yan said. "We should go back to the village."

"Should we take the moon there?" Peiyi asked.

They all looked at it. Round and glowing, it was full of a quiet tranquillity that Rendi did not wish to disturb. The others must have felt the same way, for they all nodded when MeiLan said, "I think we should leave the moon here."

"But not by itself," Peiyi said. "Who knows what will happen to it next?"

"Someone should stay with it," Widow Yan agreed.

"I will stay with it," Mr. Shan said. He looked at

Madame Chang, whose eyes had not left the moon since it had appeared. "It will not disappear again."

Rendi looked curiously at Mr. Shan. His long white beard still trickled a delicate stream of water, and the spaces between his wrinkles were few and small. But his eyes had lost their dull, absent look and now sparkled like cut crystals.

"You'll stay all night?" Rendi said.

Mr. Shan nodded. The toad, back in his familiar pocket, croaked in agreement. Mr. Shan sat down cross-legged against the moon and opened his precious book on his lap. With a look of great contentment, he began to read.

Peiyi giggled. "You look just like the sage in Madame Chang's story!" she laughed.

"What sage?" Jiming asked.

"It was a story Madame Chang told us," Rendi said. "It was about a sage who had a book with all this knowledge in it, like the secret to peace and things like that."

"Well, then, Mr. Shan," Jiming joked, "do you know the secret to peace?"

Mr. Shan looked up. His dark eyes, once confused, were now bright and wise.

"Yes," he said. "I remember everything now. The secret to peace is forgiveness."

His words hung in the air like small, ripe apples dangling from a branch. All were silent, and Mr. Shan bowed his head and began to read again.

Then Master Chao nodded at Widow Yan. Without a word, Widow Yan stepped forward, took MeiLan's hand, and placed it in Jiming's.

CHAPTER

38

The next day, when the edges of the sky began to darken like a delicate cloth soaking in ink, Peiyi burst into Madame Chang's room. Both Madame Chang and Rendi, who had been filling the lanterns with oil, looked at her in surprise.

"Madame Chang!" Peiyi cried. "You have to fix it!"

"What's wrong?" Rendi asked, alarmed.

"They think the moon should be taken to the city," Peiyi said, "and the king should figure out how to return it to the sky! And Jiming is going to be the one to take it!"

It took a moment for Rendi to untangle Peiyi's words. The "they" Peiyi mentioned was most likely the crowd of villagers downstairs. The villagers had heard the story of Jiming and the moon as if it had been told by thunder, and, one by one, they had come to the inn to discuss, argue, and decide the fate of the moon. The dining room of the inn was now completely full.

"The villagers think the moon should be brought to the king?" Rendi asked. "That is not a bad idea. Why is that a problem?"

"It's a problem because to take the moon to the king, someone has to roll it to the city!" Peiyi said. "And it's going to be Jiming! He just got home! He shouldn't leave again! Why is he leaving? Everyone leaves!"

Peiyi began to sob and then threw herself into Madame Chang's arms. Rendi stood awkwardly but looked at Madame Chang with worry.

"Peiyi," Madame Chang said, gently peeling away Peiyi's arms so she could look in her eyes. "Sometimes people must leave."

"But why?" Peiyi wept.

Madame Chang thought for a moment before she

spoke. "For the night, there is the day. For the sun, there is the moon. For people to come, people must go," she said. "It is part of the balance."

"Why do we need balance, then?" Peiyi said, her lower lip jutting out stubbornly.

"Peiyi, it's like the stories," Rendi said, trying to be helpful. "When there were too many suns, people burned. When there was no sun, people were cold. It has to be even." Then he had a sudden thought. If the sun was fire, then that meant the moon was water. Did the Village of Clear Sky, unlike everywhere else, still have water because the moon had been so near? And was there no rain because there was no moon in the sky?

"Yes," Madame Chang said, nodding. "We need balance to have harmony."

"But I don't want it to be Jiming who leaves!" Peiyi wailed.

"I know," Madame Chang said, patting her head. "And this time, he won't. Jiming will not have to leave."

"Really?" Peiyi sniffed.

"Yes," Madame Chang said. And then she added softly, but firmly, "And I will never leave. Every night of your life, I will be there for you."

She looked again into Peiyi's eyes as if trying to fill her with light. Rendi watched as Peiyi's tears disappeared and her hiccupping figure calmed into a peaceful stillness.

Madame Chang sat Peiyi softly on the bed. "I will go talk to the villagers," she said.

"What will you say?" Peiyi asked.

"The truth," Madame Chang said. "Taking the moon to the king is the wrong thing to do."

CHAPTER
39

Madame Chang left the room with Rendi following close behind. Even before they were all the way down the stairs, they could hear the voices of Master Chao, Jiming, and the villagers.

"The moon must be taken to the king immediately," a villager said. "And if the king does not know what to do, then he can take it to the emperor. The moon must return to the sky without delay!"

"Yes," another villager said. "The king or the emperor must take action at once! The moon belongs to all the people, and they are responsible for the welfare of the people. The king and the emperor are responsible for the moon!"

"They are not the only ones responsible," Jiming said in a wry tone, which Rendi could understand. Until today, the villagers had been unconcerned about the missing moon, but now, as Madame Chang and Rendi stood in the room, they were all fervent and alarmed.

"I will roll the moon to the king," Jiming continued. "But it is a long journey to the City of Far Remote, especially on foot, and it is unknown when I'll return. So before I leave, I insist that I am allowed to marry MeiLan and, in my absence, that she is treated as my honored wife."

More than anyone, Rendi could hear sorrow and the brave sadness of sacrifice in Jiming's voice. Rendi remembered the yearning in Jiming's eyes when he had been a toad. Jiming had wanted desperately to return home, but now he was leaving again.

"We can have the wedding tomorrow," Master Chao said, and all the heads in the room nodded in agreement. Except for Madame Chang's.

"Jiming should not move the moon," Madame Chang said, and they all turned to look at her. "The king can do nothing. Only a mountain can hold up the moon."

"But then it is right for Jiming to take the moon," Master Chao said in his self-important way. "Our ancestor moved a mountain. Jiming will move the moon."

"Your ancestor did not move the mountain!" Madame Chang said in a voice louder than Rendi had ever heard her use before. Madame Chang slowly looked at each villager, and one by one, each dropped his or her eyes and fell silent, overwhelmed by the force of her gaze. It was as if Madame Chang had removed a translucent veil. Her smooth, pale face seemed to illuminate the room, and Rendi again felt the awe-inspiring sensation of wishing to kneel at her feet.

"Poor villagers of Clear Sky," she said in a softer voice, "it has been so long, yet you still do not see. Your sky is not clear. Your sky is empty. Let me tell you the true story of your mountain."

THE TRUE STORY OF THE MOUNTAIN THAT MOVED

This village was once the Village of Endless Mountain, renowned for its peace and wisdom. The Moon Lady above was responsible for the peace, but the wisdom was mostly because of the sage Spirit of the Mountain, who often took the form of a human bestowing advice on those who sought him. Endless Mountain was honored and revered by all.

But time passed and people slowly began to forget about the Spirit of the Mountain and even about the Moon Lady. The villagers became thoughtless and began having small, foolish arguments. And when a new family moved to the village, none noticed the warnings of their approaching fate.

The wife and sons were loyal and humble, but the father was domineering and thoughtless. On a whim, he decided he wanted tea made from Nan Ling water and forced his sons to carry him to the Long River and stupidly risked all their lives as they rowed him into the fierce waves. If he began to lose at a game of chess, he promptly quit playing. When two baby oxen were born, he was so impatient to get them to his stable that he tied them by the tails and dragged them home. The Moon Lady and the Spirit of the Mountain looked down at him with disapproving eyes.

But one day, the man decided that the mountain, the great, never-ending mountain whose tip touched the moon, was a hindrance. "This mountain blocks my view!" he sputtered. "We must move it!"

So he gathered shovels and pails and ordered his obedient sons to dig. All day, the sons and even the wife carried away rock and dirt one bucket at a time. As the sun sank behind the mountain, the workers cast silent, pleading eyes up at the sky. So saddened by their plight, the Moon Lady entreated the Spirit of the Mountain to interfere.

The Spirit of the Mountain had barely noticed the buckets of rock that had been moved, feeling it the way one of us would feel the loss of a single hair. But the Moon Lady's appeal had roused him, and he found himself surprised and curious. Villagers had taken to watching the odd labor, some to jeer and some to encourage. But none tried to stop it. Taking human shape, the Spirit of the Mountain went to visit the man.

"Why are you trying to move the mountain?" the Spirit asked. "Why spend your every hour, every day of your life on something so meaningless?"

"This mountain of annoyance will be moved!" the man swore. "If I do not move the mountain in my lifetime, my sons will continue my work and their sons afterward, until this mountain bothers no one again! It is this stupid, unnecessary mountain that is meaningless!"

And with those words, the Mountain Spirit felt an anger build inside him, a cold, hard anger like a rock freezing in ice. The mountain was unnecessary? He was stupid and meaningless? For countless generations, the Spirit had guided and helped the villagers, and now they wished to cast him away like refuse from a chamber pot? The Spirit of the Mountain filled with bitterness and resentment. He could not stay. He would leave. The mountain would be an annoyance no longer.

The Moon Lady was alarmed, for she knew, without the mountain to anchor it, the moon could fall from the sky. But the Mountain Spirit, too angry and hurt, did not hear her words. He refused to stay where he was unwanted.

So the next morning, the Village of Endless Mountain was no longer. The never-ending mountain left, leaving behind only the flat bare stone. The land was empty, just like the sky.

"'A clear sky,' your great-grandfather said," Madame Chang told Jiming, who had listened with sudden understanding. "And this place was then called the Village of Clear Sky. But that is also when people began to leave this village, and now it is becoming empty, just like the Stone Pancake and the sky above."

"That's just all the more reason to return the moon," a villager said. "The king —"

"The king cannot do anything!" Madame Chang said, as if declaring a proclamation. She looked out at the sunset. "But everything will return. Tomorrow, at this time. Do not forget."

And with those words, Madame Chang turned and left out the back of the inn, her hair floating around her pale face so that it looked like the moon itself in a midnight cloud.

CHAPTER
40

Rendi ran out the door to follow her. Madame Chang was already walking across the Stone Pancake, her figure a silhouette against the bursting orange sky.

"Madame!" he called, but when she turned and waited for him, his mouth was as dry as a summer road. As Rendi walked with her across the flat plain, he opened and closed his mouth several times until, finally, he asked, "What happened to the Spirit of the Mountain?"

"The Spirit of the Mountain was so hurt and angry," Madame Chang said softly, as if talking to herself in a dream, "that he left his home. He wanted to leave it all behind."

Rendi looked at Madame Chang, but her eyes were as unreadable as stones as she looked off into the crimson and molten gold of the sky.

"But he carried that anger and unhappiness with him, and he could never really rest, never truly find peace," Madame Chang said. "He wandered the world, letting himself be called by many different names and acting the role of another. All he wished was to forget. Until finally, he did."

Rendi followed her gaze to where the line of the land cut the sun so that it looked like a sliced orange. They continued walking, and her pace did not slow.

"But in his quest to forget, he let himself forget everything," Madame Chang said. "Instead of losing his unhappiness, he lost himself and the things he held dearest."

With each step they took, the fire of the sun burned away and the night began to unroll across the sky like a length of black fabric.

"And we," Madame Chang said, "lost the moon."

But the moon was found and now it was before them,

its steady glow thinning the sky around it to a silver mist. Like a carved wooden statue, Mr. Shan sat cross-legged and was reading. His blue cloth bag, brought to him earlier by Madame Chang, lay limply beside him. As they approached, he looked up and met Madame Chang's eyes.

"When?" Mr. Shan asked.

"Tomorrow," she said, and Rendi looked at them both curiously, feeling as if he was at a meeting not meant for him.

But the old man looked at him, his gaze piecing and powerful but not unkind.

"Rendi," Mr. Shan said, "it is time for all of us to return."

Rendi knew that was his sign to leave, but when Madame Chang handed him a lantern to light his way back to the inn, he could not help asking another question.

"Madame Chang," Rendi asked, "why did you want me to tell stories?"

"Because I wanted to know you," Madame Chang said, "and when people tell stories, they share things about themselves."

Rendi looked into her eyes, the light in them illuminating his own thoughts.

"My stories were about me," Rendi said slowly. "Were your stories about you?"

Madame Chang smiled, put her hands on Rendi's shoulders, and touched his forehead with hers. "Goodbye, Rendi," she said softly. And then she released him into the night.

CHAPTER
41

The next morning, Rendi awoke to a sad knocking on his door. When he opened it, a tear-stained, miserable Peiyi stood in front of him.

"She lied," Peiyi said, her lip trembling as a fresh tear rolled down her cheek.

"Who lied?" Rendi asked.

"Madame Chang!" Peiyi said, a sob threatening to take over. "She's gone! She left! Even though she promised!"

Rendi rushed to Madame Chang's room. Peiyi was right. Madame Chang was gone. The room was empty except for the beams of the sun that draped themselves on the carved wooden table and bed. Peiyi joined Rendi at the door, and they both stood, staring.

"I can't believe it," Rendi said, his voice as hollow as he felt inside. Even though the villagers had largely disregarded Madame Chang's words after she had left the inn, he had believed her. But now she was gone.

"Can't believe what?" Jiming's voice said behind them. They both turned and looked up at Jiming, dejected.

"Madame Chang left," Peiyi said, tears threatening again. Without Madame Chang, Jiming's departure was now certain.

"Hmm." Jiming frowned as he glanced at the bare room. "Did she pay her bill?"

"Yes!" Rendi said indignantly. "She even paid in advance!"

"Well, then it's nothing to get gloomy about," Jiming said in a jolly tone. "Sometimes people have to leave."

"But..." Peiyi started.

"Come on, baby sister!" Jiming said, swinging Peiyi up in the air. "No sad faces! Your brother is getting married today!"

In spite of herself, Peiyi laughed. Jiming had to leave as well, but he had obviously decided to enjoy the day as much as possible. Peiyi landed on the floor, and Rendi watched as she set her face into a grim smile. He knew she was determined not to spoil Jiming's day.

The whole village was attending the wedding, and the day was full of hectic activity. Rendi was sent hurrying back and forth for water while Jiming and Master Chao butchered a pig for the evening's wedding banquet. Peiyi was sent to help MeiLan, who was frantically sewing.

"We're breaking many traditions," Widow Yan said, shaking her head as Master Chao, Jiming, and Rendi brought over tea and wine as betrothal gifts. "No matchmaker, no bridal cakes! We don't even know if this is an auspicious day!"

"It's auspicious," Jiming said. "Any day I get married is auspicious!"

They all laughed, but underneath the laughter there was a stream of sadness. When Rendi brought some red thread for Peiyi and MeiLan's sewing, he saw a silver tear sneak out of the corner of Peiyi's eye. As the tear fell, it made an unnoticed stain on the crimson silk, like a drop of blood. Rendi frowned. Where was Madame Chang? Had she really left? It was impossible! Yet "Goodbye," she had said. And he remembered the solemn finality of her farewell, like the tolling of a bell. But what about the moon? And Mr. Shan?

Rendi sidled next to Peiyi. "As soon as I can," he said to her in a low voice, "I'm going to go out to Mr. Shan. He'll know what happened to Madame Chang. Maybe she left a message with him."

Peiyi's face filled with sudden hope, and she nodded. "Yes! He'll know! Maybe she went to get something or..." Peiyi trailed off, unable to imagine why Madame Chang would leave. For a moment, Peiyi and Rendi stared at each other, both at a loss. Then Peiyi nodded again at Rendi and returned to her sewing.

But Rendi could not leave. Master Chao and Jiming kept him in a rush without a moment of rest. When Rendi was sent to hire the sedan chair and musicians, he tried to protest.

"MeiLan lives right next door!" Rendi said. "Why do you need a wedding procession to get her? It'll be the shortest parade ever!"

"We'll make a couple of circles on the Stone Pancake," Jiming said in a jolly tone. "The whole village is coming out. We're going to make it a celebration at sunset!"

Rendi tried again.

"I should go out and check up on Mr. Shan, though," he said. "He watched the moon all day yesterday, and no one has seen him at all today."

"He'll be all right," Master Chao said. "We gave him enough food and wine to last a week. It is too bad he will miss the wedding, but someone must watch the moon."

"And," Jiming said, a grimness creeping into his grin, "he will not have to watch the moon for much longer, anyway."

Rendi's tasks were finally finished when the sun hung above the horizon like a golden peach ready to fall. Villagers gathered before Master Chao's inn and lit firecrackers, loud and deafening, as the rented bridal sedan arrived.

Jiming, dressed in his finest, inspected the red embroidered silk canopy and the costumed carriers with mock discipline.

"Only the best to pick up my bride!" he said.

As Jiming and the villagers joked and laughed, Peiyi found her way to Rendi's side.

"Did you see Mr. Shan?" she hissed at him.

Rendi shook his head. "Not yet," he whispered. He looked at the crowd all around him. "I'll go now."

Peiyi, too, looked at the crowd and nodded at him. She began to cheer loud enough for two, and he scurried away, both of them hoping their questions could be answered by the old man by the moon.

CHAPTER

42

It was late in the day, and the air had cooled slightly. As Rendi walked quickly across the stone plain, a tender breeze stroked the earth, and the sun seemed to have softened its glare. There was still no rain, however, and the snail shells Rendi had dropped were brittle and dry.

And the questions in his head seemed to repeat with every step he took. Where was Madame Chang? Why did she leave? Was Peiyi right? Had Madame Chang lied to them?

A purple curtain began to drape over the sky, and

Rendi's thoughts stopped him in midstride. He didn't believe Madame Chang had lied. She would not lie. She could not. All that he knew of her told him that her words were always pure and true. For her to lie was impossible. As impossible, Rendi thought grimly, as the moon falling from the sky.

He continued walking, and instead of thinking of Madame Chang, he began to think of Mr. Shan. Last night, Mr. Shan had looked at him with clear eyes full of endless wisdom, and Rendi began to feel hopeful confidence bubble inside him, like a flowing spring. Mr. Shan knew how to end the argument of the snails and how to save him from Fang and Liu. He seemed to know the answers to everything. Mr. Shan would know the answers now too.

However, as the tall tree came into sight, Rendi did not see what he had expected. There was no Mr. Shan sitting cross-legged reading his book with the toad croaking in his pocket, and there was no round, pearl-like moon glowing behind him. Where was Mr. Shan? Where was the moon? Rendi's pace quickened to a run.

"Mr. Shan!" Rendi called. "Where's the moon? Mr. Shan?"

Rendi was asking his questions to the sky, for only the soft breeze answered him. He darted to the tree, trying to will his eyes to lie to him.

But the place where Mr. Shan and the moon had sat was completely bare, except for two copper coins.

CHAPTER

43

Rendi held the two copper coins in his hand. How many times had he seen Mr. Shan jingle these same coins in front of the toad? Rendi collapsed against the tree, tears wetting his eyes. Mr. Shan and Madame Chang were truly gone.

But what about the moon? And the toad? He heard a faint croaking by the lake. Rendi slowly walked toward the bridge.

Had Mr. Shan and Madame Chang left together? Had they taken the moon with them? Maybe this was how

Madame Chang planned to keep Jiming from leaving, by taking the moon instead. Mr. Shan was surprisingly strong, Rendi knew—perhaps he was rolling it now. Another croak came from the lake, in the shadows of the bridge.

Rendi peered under the bridge, kneeling on the damp bank.

"Toad! Toad!" Rendi called, and then grinned, remembering Mr. Shan's pet name for it. "Rabbit!"

As Rendi moved closer, a strange thought came to him. In Madame Chang's story, the old sage transformed a tadpole into a baby rabbit. Had that tadpole been a baby toad? Could that rabbit turn back into a toad? Was that why Mr. Shan gave his toad such an odd name? Rendi wrinkled his brow and called again, "Rabbit! Are you there, Rabbit?"

The rippling water cast a flashing light into the shadows, and Rendi saw a small green frog. It wasn't Mr. Shan's toad. But there was something. Above the green frog, there was a strange outline in the stone.

The lake glimmered in the setting sun, and the flickering, reflecting light was barely enough for Rendi to see under the bridge. The frog hopped away, but Rendi leaned out farther, squinting. Was it? Yes, on the underside of the stone bridge there were two deep indentations. They were in the shape of hands. Rendi lifted his own hands in imitation. Those handprints pressed in the stone looked as if they had been made by someone holding up the bridge. Mr. Shan's handprints!

And just as Rendi realized this—*splash!*—he slipped and fell into the lake.

The soft, silver waves caught him gently and embraced him with warm arms. His clothes spread from him like an expanding flower, and as the water swirled, a confusing mix of memories flooded through him.

Only a mountain can hold up the moon, Madame Chang had said, looking out into the orange sky. *At this time. Do not forget.*

A celebration at sunset, Jiming had said, laughing, *A parade on the Stone Pancake!*

It is time for all of us to return, Mr. Shan had said, the great, glowing moon behind him. *You should go.*

Then, a powerful current, like an invisible hand, curled underneath Rendi and pushed him upward until he burst through the surface of the lake, gasping. He dragged himself to the shore, his mind racing and repeating, *It is time. You should go. It is time.* He looked again at Mr. Shan's handprints on the bottom of the bridge.

"Only a mountain can hold up the moon," Rendi whispered. He looked at the violet sky, and the sun beginning to slip behind the horizon. Ignoring the heaviness of his dripping clothes, Rendi began to run.

CHAPTER

44

Rendi raced across the Stone Pancake, droplets of water flying from him like silver seeds. He ran as if he were one of WangYi's shot arrows, and his feet scarcely touched the ground. His thoughts matched his quick steps. Could the mountain be...? If they returned at sunset...? Would the wedding parade on the Stone Pancake...? If so, how could he...? Even though Rendi could not even ask himself the full questions, he began to form a plan in his mind.

The sky above had turned a dusky purple, and the last

slice of the sun radiated its rainbow of gold. In the distance, Rendi saw a parade of people and heard the dim noise of celebration. The bridal sedan with its red silk canopy brighter than a rooster's crown was like a flaming peony on the stone. Rendi dashed toward it.

The raucous music and laughter paused in surprise as the people saw the strange, half-drowned figure of a boy running toward them. The sedan carriers stopped their march in shock as Rendi, barely recognizable with his wet and disheveled appearance, barreled toward the bridal sedan and split through the curtains of the canopy.

"Rendi?" MeiLan gasped, raising her hand in disbelief. She looked very beautiful, shimmering in her red silk dress, which was even more brilliant than the sedan chair, and her golden hairpins glittered in the dying sunlight. But it was the exquisite green jade bracelet that Rendi grabbed. With a quick motion, he slipped it off her delicate wrist and popped out of the sedan.

"My bracelet!" Rendi heard MeiLan cry out. He took a quick glance behind him and saw she had done as he hoped. *I will not get married without it*, MeiLan had said about her bracelet, and she had meant it. Because without hesitation, she had jumped out of the bridal chair and ran after him. The wedding parade, completely astonished, all began to chase the bride.

Rendi ran faster and faster, faster than if he were a thief trying to escape, faster than if there were a Noxious Toad behind him. MeiLan shouted, and he could make out the yells of Master Chao, Jiming, and Peiyi from the din that followed her. But he continued to run. He ran as far from the Stone Pancake as he could, over the mounds of dirt that covered the dried-up well and Fang's forgotten belongings, through the garden of snails, past the line of firefly lanterns, and down the street away from the inn.

But on the dry, dusty road, his legs began to falter, and MeiLan's voice grew louder in his ears. The sky dimmed darker and darker, the blackness of night pouring toward the earth as if from an overturned bowl. Rendi tried to keep running, but MeiLan's fingertips clutched his flapping, damp shirt and . . .

BOOM!

A deafening, piercing crash like thunder echoed across the village. Louder than the wedding firecrackers or

Magistrate Tiger's roars, louder than even Jiming's burp as a toad, the noise seemed to split the sky. Houses rocked, trees swayed, and all the villagers—Rendi and MeiLan included—fell to the ground. The ground trembled. Lanterns, fireflies, and stars disappeared, and for one moment, all was black and silent.

Then, "Look!" Peiyi said, her soft voice as loud as a yell in the stillness.

She pointed toward the sky, but her words and motions were unneeded. Everyone was looking. They were staring and gaping, wide-eyed and speechless.

Behind the Inn of Clear Sky, a mountain had grown. A never-ending mountain whose tip stretched high, so high into the sky that it touched the moon. For the moon had returned. It was above, a glowing pearl bathing all of them with light.

"The moon!" someone whispered. "The mountain!" and the voice broke into a smothered sob of joy. All of them stood breathless, drinking in the sight they hadn't realized they had been so thirsty for. The pure light of the moon cascaded upon them, reshaping and filling them until Rendi felt transformed and bursting. He glanced at the row of villagers, at MeiLan, Jiming, Master Chao, Peiyi, and Widow Yan. Their eyes were large and luminous, and a wetness spilled onto his cheeks.

But was he crying? Because at that moment, the sky brightened with tiny, twinkling lights as if hundreds of lanterns and firecrackers were lit in celebration, and sparkling drops of water sprinkled from the sky.

It was raining. It was a gentle, soft rain that kissed the earth. The dry grass, leaves, and people eagerly stretched upward, reaching to catch the happy, laughing tears from the mountain and the moon.

CHAPTER

45

It was crisp and cool the next evening as Rendi walked down the road. Billowing violet clouds were edged with pink and gold as the sun made its farewell. Small blades of grass, already green, had sprouted through the stones and made a soft carpet for his feet. His bag, slung over his shoulder, was not light but easily carried. He smiled at himself proudly, remembering his weak, feeble arms when he had first arrived at the inn. Now he felt strong and able to carry almost any burden.

"Rendi! Rendi!" A small figure ran after him. He

turned and gave a crooked smile. Peiyi was going to say goodbye after all. When he had made his farewells to the others, she had closed herself in her room and refused to come out and he had had to say goodbye to her through her door. But perhaps that was better, because now she was glaring at him.

"You're really leaving!" Peiyi said accusingly. "After everything! After saving all of us when the mountain came back, after seeing the moon and the rain come again! Now you're leaving! Everyone leaves!"

Rendi's bag suddenly felt heavier. Peiyi reminded him so much of his sister, and his chest filled with both remorse and longing.

"It's time for me to go," he said, and then he remembered Madame Chang's words. "Sometimes people must leave."

"But why you?" Peiyi said, crossing her arms.

"Before, I didn't leave right. I was angry. I have my own family . . . I have to go home . . ." Rendi started, but he confused himself with his own explanation. Finally he said, "Right now, I'm not leaving. I'm returning."

Peiyi sniffed, her lower lip sticking out, but the hard line of her shoulders softened.

"You know that Madame Chang didn't lie to you," Rendi said, "don't you?"

They both looked up at the deepening blue sky, the pale moon already above and watching. Across the Starry River, a reddish-orange light, the color of a rooster's comb, streaked from the departing sun straight toward the moon.

"I know," Peiyi said, her eyes staying on the moon. Rendi swallowed, but the sad weight upon him lessened. He took his bag from his shoulder and opened it.

"Here," Rendi said. "This is for you."

He handed Peiyi his rice bowl. The gold had been all but rubbed away, but the fine blue-and-white porcelain gleamed in the moonlight, and the creamy whiteness was as smooth as the inside of a shell. In Peiyi's hands, the painted rabbit seemed to tremble.

"Rendi," Peiyi whispered, her voice tremulous, "is this the emperor's... Magistrate Tiger's...? I can't take this!"

"It's a gift," Rendi said, grinning. All of a sudden, he felt as light as a butterfly. He reached into his bag and pulled out Mr. Shan's two copper coins and dropped them into the bowl, laughing. "If you can't take it, give it to

Jiming and MeiLan! They can give it to their first child, and their child can pass it on to their children, and the bowl will go on forever and ever!"

"A wedding gift?" Peiyi said, still awed and unsure. Her fingers ran around the thin, delicate edge of the bowl, making a round circle.

"No," Rendi said, suddenly serious. He looked into Peiyi's eyes as Madame Chang had looked into his that last night. "It's a thank-you gift."

Peiyi gazed back, suddenly full of wisdom beyond her years. She gave a small nod and then, unexpectedly, threw her arms around Rendi in a rough hug, her face buried in his chest.

Then, without another word, she pushed herself away, turned, and ran. Rendi watched as she ran down the moon path back to the inn, the Inn of Never-Ending Mountain, stopping only once to wave goodbye.

He watched her small figure disappear and brought the bag back to his shoulder to continue onward. But before he took another step, he looked at the tall mountain that touched the moon, its peak soaring into the sky as if holding it up. Misty clouds draped softly, but up where the mountain met the moon, Rendi thought he could still see what he expected to be there.

There was old Mr. Shan, the Spirit of the Mountain, who sat at the mountain's tip with the book in his lap. The three-legged toad hopped next to him. At least, it was the three-legged toad part of the time, because it kept transforming into a jade-white rabbit. As it jumped up and down, it calmly changed back and forth. Toad. Rabbit. Toad.

Above them, thousands of stars circled the moon, like twinkling fish leaping and dancing to a song of harmony that only they could hear. Madame Chang, the Moon Lady, having finished granting their secret wishes, now waited as the Celestial Rooster streaked across the sky carrying her husband, WangYi, to her. The moonlit clouds floated as if on gentle waves of water.

In the shimmering, silver light, Rendi smiled up at all of them. They were all at home, all at peace, and finally all returned to the Starry River of the Sky.

AUTHOR'S NOTE

As I mentioned in my author's note in *Where the Mountain Meets the Moon* (this book's companion), I spent most of my childhood resisting my parents' efforts to teach me about our heritage. It was only when I grew older that I began to value what I had learned and mourned what I had not. So, as an adult, I tried to rediscover my roots by visiting Taiwan, China, and Hong Kong. During those travels, I found myself creating stories inspired by Chinese myths I had read in my childhood.

These new stories permeated my soul and consumed my thoughts. All stories authors write, regardless of the inspirations, characters, or settings, are personal. At least they are for me. And my journey to write this book was much like Rendi's—starting with confusion and doubt and ending with wonder, strength, and self-discovery.

When I began writing, I worried that, as an Americanized Asian, some might think I had no right to reinterpret these Chinese folktales with my own modern sensibilities (disregarding historical details such as foot-binding, for example). Many might be offended that the myths were changed or altered at all. My worries made me hesitant to continue.

But then I remembered my travels. During my trips to Asia, I visited many temples, all of them still used for worship. I was struck by the paper offerings being burned there. Instead of just the traditional paper ghost money, paper replicas of computers, cell phones, and even electric toothbrushes were now being set ablaze. I realized that people had allowed their customs to change. The tradition had grown to fit the modern world.

I thought this was fascinating and wonderful — how myths and beliefs are and can be transformed over time. Somehow, to me, it made these beliefs more real, more "living." And suddenly, I saw that the Asian culture was just like the characteristics that are attributed to bamboo — strong and flexible. My small adaptations would be at worst harmless and at best a new fresh sprout — and neither could injure the original stalk.

So, with those thoughts, I found peace to continue writing my stories and this book. Obviously, my intent has never been to replace the traditional retellings of Chinese folklore — in fact, I hope my book makes those unfamiliar with the tales curious to read them. For those who already know the mythology, I hope that prior knowledge only makes my version more enjoyable. However, for all readers, my not-so-secret wish is that this book gives you the same wonder, faith, and peace that writing it gave me.

Some of the books that inspired
STARRY RIVER OF THE SKY

Asiapac Editorial. *Origins of Chinese Music*. Singapore: Asiapac Books, 2007.

Asiapac Editorial. *Origins of Chinese Tea and Wine*. Singapore: Asiapac Books, 2004.

Carpenter, Frances. *Tales of a Chinese Grandmother*. Rutland, VT: Tuttle Publishing, 1973.

Conover, Sarah and Chen Hui. *Harmony: A Treasury of Chinese Wisdom for Children and Parents*. Spokane and Cheney, WA: Eastern Washington University Press, 2008.

Fang, Linda. *The Ch'i-lin Purse: A Collection of Ancient Chinese Stories*. New York: Farrar, Straus and Giroux, 1995.

The Frog Rider—Folk Tales from China (First Series). Beijing: Foreign Languages Press, 1980.

Han, Carolyn. *Tales from Within the Clouds: Nakhi Stories of China*. Translated by Jaiho Cheng. Honolulu, HI: University of Hawai'i Press, 1997.

Hume, Lotta Carswell. *Favorite Children's Stories from China and Tibet*. Rutland, VT: Tuttle Publishing, 1962.

Kendall, Carol and Yao-wen Li. *Sweet and Sour: Tales from China*. New York: Clarion Books, 1978.

Lin, Adet. *The Milky Way and Other Chinese Folk Tales*. New York: Harcourt, Brace & World, Inc., 1961.

Lobb, Fred H. *The Wonderful Treasure Horse: Mongolian, Manchu and Turkic Folktales from China*. Xlibris Corp., 2000.

Various. *Folk Tales of the West Lake*. N.p.: Olympia Press, 2007.

Werner, E.T.C. *Myths and Legends of China*. Mineola, NY: Dover Publications, 1994.

Yip, Mingmei. *Chinese Children's Favorite Stories*. Rutland, VT: Tuttle Publishing, 2004.

Yuan, Haiwang. *The Magic Lotus Lantern and Other Tales from the Han Chinese*. Westport, CT: Libraries Unlimited, 2006.

A PEEK BEHIND THE SCENES AT GRACE LIN'S SKETCHBOOK

ENTERING THE VILLAGE OF CLEAR SKY

THE DAY OF FIVE POISONS

CATCHING FIREFLIES

PEIYI READY TO SAVE THE DAY

THE GIANT TOAD

RENDI SAYS GOODBYE

TURN THE PAGE FOR A PEEK
AT THE COMPANION NOVEL TO
STARRY RIVER OF THE SKY.

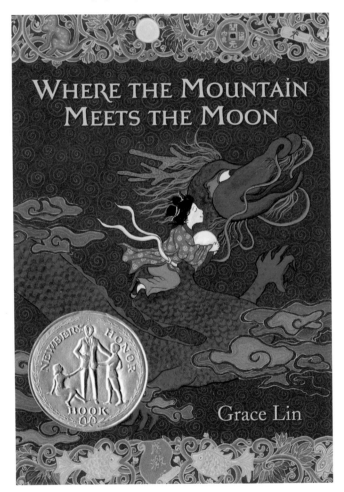

WHERE THE MOUNTAIN
MEETS THE MOON

Grace Lin

AVAILABLE NOW!

CHAPTER

1

Far away from here, following the Jade River, there was once a black mountain that cut into the sky like a jagged piece of rough metal. The villagers called it Fruitless Mountain because nothing grew on it and birds and animals did not rest there.

Crowded in the corner of where Fruitless Mountain and the Jade River met was a village that was a shade of faded brown. This was because the land around the village was hard and poor. To coax rice out of the stubborn land, the fields had to be flooded with water. The villagers had to tramp in the mud, bending and stooping and planting day after day. Working in the mud so much made it spread everywhere and the hot sun dried it onto their clothes and hair and homes. Over time, everything in the village had become the dull color of dried mud.

One of the houses in this village was so small that its wood boards, held together by the roof, made one think of a bunch of matches tied with a piece of twine. Inside, there was barely enough room for three people to sit around the table — which was lucky because only three people lived there. One of them was a young girl called Minli.

Minli was not brown and dull like the rest of the village. She had glossy black hair with pink cheeks, shining eyes always eager for adventure, and a fast smile that flashed from her face. When people saw her lively and impulsive spirit, they thought her name, which meant *quick thinking,* suited her well. "Too well," her mother sighed, as Minli had a habit of quick acting as well.

Ma sighed a great deal, an impatient noise usually accompanied with a frown at their rough clothes, rundown house, or meager food. Minli could not remember a time when Ma did not sigh; it often made Minli wish she had been called a name that meant *gold* or *fortune* instead. Because Minli and her parents, like the village and the land around them, were very poor. They were barely able to harvest enough rice to feed themselves, and the only money in the house was two old copper coins that sat in a blue rice bowl with a white rabbit painted on it. The coins and the bowl belonged to Minli; they had been given to her when she was a baby, and she had had them for as long as she could remember.

What kept Minli from becoming dull and brown like the rest of the village were the stories her father told her every night at dinner. She glowed with such wonder and excitement that even Ma would smile, though she would shake her head at the same time. Ba seemed to drop his gray and work weariness — his black eyes sparkled like raindrops in the sun when he began a story.

"Ba, tell me the story about Fruitless Mountain again," Minli would say as her mother spooned their plain rice into bowls. "Tell me again why nothing grows on it."

"Ah," Minli's father said, "you've heard this so many times. You know."

"Tell me again, Ba," Minli begged. "Please."

"Okay," he said, and as he set down his chopsticks his smile twinkled in a way that Minli loved.

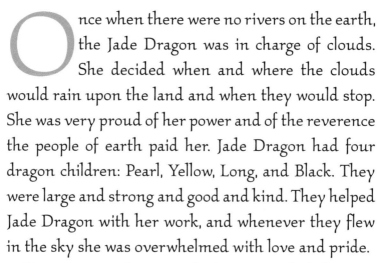

THE STORY OF FRUITLESS MOUNTAIN

Once when there were no rivers on the earth, the Jade Dragon was in charge of clouds. She decided when and where the clouds would rain upon the land and when they would stop. She was very proud of her power and of the reverence the people of earth paid her. Jade Dragon had four dragon children: Pearl, Yellow, Long, and Black. They were large and strong and good and kind. They helped Jade Dragon with her work, and whenever they flew in the sky she was overwhelmed with love and pride.

However, one day, as Jade Dragon ended the rain and moved the clouds away from the land, she overheard some villagers' conversation.

"Ah, thank goodness the rain is gone," one man said.

"Yes," another said, "I'm so tired of the rain. I'm glad the clouds are gone and the sun is finally shining."

Those words filled Jade Dragon with anger. Tired of rain! Glad the clouds were gone! Jade Dragon was indignant. How dare the villagers dishonor her that way!

Jade Dragon was so offended that she decided that she would never let it rain again. "The people can enjoy the sun forever," Jade Dragon thought resentfully.

Of course, that meant despair for the people on earth. As the sun beat overhead and the rain never came, drought and famine spread over the land. Animals and trees withered and died and the people begged for rain, but Jade Dragon ignored them.

But their suffering did not go unnoticed by Jade Dragon's children. They were horrified at the anguish and misery on earth. One by one, they went to their mother and pleaded forgiveness for the humans — but even their words did not soften their mother's cold heart. "We will never make it rain for the people again," Jade Dragon vowed.

Pearl, Yellow, Long, and Black met in secret.

"We must do something to help the people," Black said. "If they do not get water soon, they will all die."

"Yes," Yellow said, "but what can we do? We cannot make it rain. We cannot dishonor Mother with disobedience."

Long looked down at the earth. "I will sacrifice myself for the people of earth," he said. "I will lie on the land and transform myself into water for them to drink."

The others looked at him in astonishment, but one by one they nodded.

"I will do the same," Yellow said.

"As will we," Pearl and Black said.

So Jade Dragon's children went down to earth and turned themselves into water, saving the people on the earth. They became the four great rivers of the land, stopping the drought and death of all those on earth.

But when Jade Dragon saw what her children had done, she cursed herself for her pride. No longer would her dragon children fly in the air with her or call her Mother. Her heart broke in grief and sadness; she fell from the sky and turned herself into the Jade River in hopes that she could somehow be reunited with her children.

Fruitless Mountain is the broken heart of Jade Dragon. Nothing grows or lives on the mountain; the land around it is hard and the water of the river is dark because Jade Dragon's sad spirit is still there. Until Jade Dragon is no longer lonely and is reunited with at least one of her children, Fruitless Mountain will remain bare.

Vigor Photo Studio

GRACE LIN is the award-winning author and illustrator of *The Year of the Dog*, *The Year of the Rat*, and *Dumpling Days*. *Where the Mountain Meets the Moon* and *Starry River of the Sky* were partially inspired by Grace's travels to Beijing, Shanghai, Hong Kong, and Taipei, where this photo (also an inspired fantasy) was taken. Grace lives in Massachusetts. Her website is www.gracelin.com.

★ "REMARKABLE."
—*Booklist* (starred review)

"GENTLE, APPEALING . . . ENGAGING." —*Kirkus Reviews*

"HUMOROUS AND THOUGHTFUL."
—*School Library Journal*

A Newbery Honor Book
A *New York Times* bestseller
A *Today* show Al's Book Club for Kids pick

★ "TIMELESS."
—*Booklist* (starred review)